\KA·TAS·TRO·PHE\

The Dramatic Actions of Kat Morgan

Hidden Angel Series

Other books by Sylvia M. DeSantis

Watercharms: Ocean-Reiki Meditations
(2011, Schiffer Pub Ltd.)

Academic Apartheid: Waging the Adjunct War
(2012, Cambridge Scholars Publishing)

\KA·TAS·TRO·PHE\

Sylvia M. Desantis

Hidden Angel Series

atmosphere press

*In memory of Dr. J.D. Stahl (1952–2010),
wonderful professor, kind thesis advisor,
and gifted scholar. You made studying YA lit
more than just acceptable; you made it legitimate.*

Angels never know it's time
To close the book and gracefully decline.
—Banks and Rutherford

PREFACE

"Lil! Over here!" Lily Caleno turns to see her best friend and colleague, Dane, waving from a deep copse of trees. Dressed in oxblood jeans, a black sweater, and loafers, Dane looks stylish and handsome, hot even. Lily looks down at her own skinny jeans and Hunter boots while running a quick hand through her curls, and nods. Yeah, she and Dane are pulling it off just fine. If Ace has complaints, it won't be about their ability to blend in.

Dane wanders out from the trees, stepping around fallen branches and mulchy grass. "This is ruining my Italian loafers," he says, wrinkling his face in distaste.

"It'll be fine," Lily says. "This never takes long." As Lily and Dane walk slowly beside the dense tree line, they startle a blanket of birds that flutter into the high branches that make up the thick canopy. Crunching over dead leaves, Lily moves into a break between the rough, ashy trees and into a clearing of evergreens. Dane follows silently. Their breath puffs bright against the lush path. Lily catches a whiff of sandalwood and cedar, sensing Ace before she sees him.

Around a short bend he sits on an ancient iron bench tucked into a forgotten corner, face lifted to the watery sun with eyes closed. Lily takes in the black jacket, pants, and motorcycle boots along with his jet-black hair, loose curls pulled into a ponytail. All of it just right.

"Hello, Lily. Dane." Ace smiles and opens his eyes while Lily and Dane simultaneously drop to one knee. Even if the ancient rules did not require a show of obedience, Lily and Dane, fallen stars gravitating around their perfect sun, would willingly bow before Ace's greatness. Some angels just command respect without demanding it.

Lily takes a deep breath, inhaling Ace's spicy scent.

"Welcome, Angelicus," says Ace. At these words the three angels stand and embrace. Ace gestures for Lily and Dane to take a seat next to him on the peeling bench. Although Lily knows Ace well, his eyes always startle her, a blue so thick they appear black.

"You both look well. I like the clothing, the demeanor. Nicely done."

Lily smiles at the compliment. "Thanks."

"Since you've already received your glyphs and should be ready for your undertaking," Ace says as Dane and Lily both nod in agreement, "you will now manifest completely into the human world. *Züsnorum nom kashmirz*, my angels."

Lily leans forward, confused. "Wait. What else did the Council say?" Why are they being sent off without the rest of the instructions? There *must* be more, especially after the Seattle disaster. Beside her Dane smirks.

"You don't need further instructions," Ace says quietly.

Lily frowns. "Usually I would agree, but this group...Ace, I've got a girl who cuts, another who won't eat, Dane is convinced the one boy is building a bomb..."

"Dane thinks all kids are making bombs."

"True," Dane snorts and nods.

"Yeah, but this time I actually agree with him. And there's this lacrosse player..."

"I know all about them," Ace says, not unkindly. He stands, his eyes reflecting the clouds scudding over the sun. "Lily, this is your universe. Make it spin."

When Lily blinks, Ace is gone, a few blood-red feathers fluttering through the air.

ONE

I position the beaker in front of me, crack the egg, and start to separate the white while holding the yolk in the shell. This is harder than it looks, and I end up with egg everywhere. The next step of the experiment involves adding a strong acid to the egg white protein. Around me everyone cracks eggs, pours acid, and makes frantic notes. Even though I'd rather just do this myself, I realize there's no way I can.

"Hey, Joey, can you add the acid? I'll stir while you pour." Joey lifts an eyebrow at Taylor and saunters back to our workbench. Joey Lawlor had been joking with Taylor Schmidt about that Saturday's Head of the Schuylkill, the biggest regatta in Philly all year. Even kids uninterested in the rowing scene at Marshall know Joey and Taylor are two of our best rowers.

"Hey, I heard that guy from St. Paul's broke his leg. Probably out for the season. Sucks for him!"

"Yeah! Sucks for him!" Taylor mimics Joey, pumping the air like an idiot and almost knocking over a Bunsen burner. Last season St. Paul's papered our boats and all the rigging the night before one of our biggest races. This supposedly got their team a week of detention but it didn't stop them from winning the Varsity Eight race by half a seat.

I don't care about any of that anymore, but it was important to me once.

Taylor checks himself out and takes a selfie in front of one of the wavy glass-fronted cabinets in the back of the lab while Shelley Dunlap, Taylor's lab partner, rolls her eyes so hard it looks like it hurts.

Joey grabs the test tube hard enough to make it slosh over the pitted table and some of my lab notes. As he begins to pour, the egg white gets kind of chunky.

"Ok, good." I check my notes and nod.

"That's all it does?"

"Well, yeah. The acid is breaking the hydrogen bonds. That's what Miss Clarick said should happen." I make a few calculations on our lab sheet and look up. "Hey, what are you doing? Joey, don't." My stomach clenches into hard knots as Joey grabs a packet of sugar, a beaker of leftover potassium nitrate, and some vinegar. "Kat, you are so uptight. You need to *relax*." He snickers as he stirs it over the flame he's cranked up. I ball my hands into fists and step back, trying to keep it together. If I blow this lab report, my parents will kill me.

Chemistry, physics...I like classes where one action very clearly and distinctly leads to an equally rational reaction. I'm not, however, so stellar in math, a problem my parents never let me forget. Amber says that math works rationally too, if I'd just give it a chance, but I don't think so. If you muck something up in a science experiment you can just look at the hypothesis, backtrack, figure out what went wrong, and start again. I wish life was more like that.

"Kat? Joey? What's going on?" Miss Clarick's voice sounds like shattered glass across the room, especially when she's mad. Thick white smoke billows from our beaker in a huge plume. As Clarick heads over, squishing on gummy-soled shoes that look about a hundred years old, I wave my hands frantically and try to blow away the smoke from our renegade beaker.

"What have you done? What's this mess?" Clarick's

glare makes me so nervous I forget I've shoved my sleeves to my elbow to start mopping up the white ash settling on our workbench when she tsk-tsks me. "Kat, what happened to your arms? *Kat?*"

"Nothing, Miss Clarick," I say automatically, struggling to pull down my sleeves as fast as possible without getting the mess all over my hoodie. Clarick stands there, hands on hips, glaring through tiny little round glasses that make her watery eyes look huge and stoned.

"Oh, man, Miss Clarick, I don't know what happened!" Joey slides his phone into his back pocket and puts on his best teacher face, the one that gets him out of detention. Even creaky old antiques like Clarick find it irresistible. It makes me want to barf.

"Clean this up," she spits at both of us, but mostly me. "*Now.*" She narrows her huge owl eyes and *dammit* steals a look at my covered arms. "Kat, you'll see me after class."

"Yes, Miss Clarick." As she squish-squashes away, I turn to Joey. "Are you *trying* to screw our grade?"

The fact that I'm super pissed doesn't even register. "Dude, that was sick! Did you see her face?" Mercifully, the bell rings. I grit my teeth, pack my books, and shove some gum into my mouth, anything to keep from reaching out and slapping the snot out of him.

"Whatever." I wipe off our smeared lab sheet and stuff it into my messenger. Fabulous. I'm sure we'll be getting another *stellar* grade. I hate Joey. He never listens to me. He doesn't hear me at all.

When you denature protein, according to Miss Clarick, you break bonds. I wouldn't call the experiment a complete failure since that's what happened, just not exactly in the way Miss Clarick, or anybody, was expecting.

The situation with my arms, with Joey, and with my life in general is not something I am even remotely interested in sharing with Hunter. Too bad though because an hour later I'm in our principal, Mr. Hunter's, office sitting across from him and next to Mrs. Bonsky, our ancient school counselor, trying to convince them there's nothing wrong.

"My cat scratched me. She's, like, out of control. Really, it's no big deal." Hunter looks suspicious, but it might just be the way the fluorescent lights glare off his bald head. Bonsky is harder to read, but looks skeptical. I hold my sleeves bunched in my fists while I kick my Docs against the floor and pick fuzz from my tights.

"Miss Clarick suggested they were very *regular* scratches. Covered in scabs?" I love it when people, especially teachers, end their statements like they're asking a question. Very confidence-inspiring. I chew my cheek and keep my mouth shut.

Mrs. Bonsky looks like someone's grandma, with poufy white hair and very straight white teeth that have to be fake. I want to tell her to butt out, that she really won't get it, but I almost feel bad. She's been cool, like supporting the campaign to get seniors their own study hall space and getting the soda machines put back in the south hallway. *Still, this is not your business, Bonsky.* I try not to look nasty. She sighs deeply and I smell the mint she's just popped in her mouth.

Bonsky leans in towards me as Hunter sits back, making his chair groan. Full-bellied and out of patience, Hunter might have once been an okay teacher, but it's obvious he's sick of kids. He rests his dusty grey eyes on me and fiddles with a class ring that looks tight and uncomfortable on his thick finger.

"What's going on, Kat." His eyes look flat, like slate. It's not really a question.

"Nothing." I shrug. "Joey kind of, eh, made a mess with the experiment but we totally cleaned it up."

"Now I *think*," Mrs. Bonksy smiles towards the desk, "Principal Hunter is asking about those scratches on your arm. Or, hmmm, maybe your classes? Principal Hunter?" I cough back a laugh watching Hunter try not to roll his eyes. I can get ahead of this.

"My cat is really more of a kitten, and sometimes she really just goes bonkers." I wait a beat to see if they're biting. "Last week she was climbing the curtains in the living room, and I went to get her down and got some scratches." Hunter raises one hairy eyebrow and then rubs his face with his huge bear paw of a hand.

"Kat," he says, looking down and flipping through a pile of papers in a folder, "Mrs. Bonsky has brought some irregularities in your record to my attention." Okay, then. I know where this is going.

"You're not in trouble, dear," Bonsky rushes to assure me, reaching over to put a papery hand on my arm, "we just want to discuss some things."

Hunter clears his throat. "Your academics seem a little...sporadic," he grunts as he flips open my file. One long fan of bright pink hair falls in my eyes and I leave it there. Why do teachers always think they know what's happening? Let's be honest. Most of them don't know shit about it.

"You had been in our Young Scholars Program

through last spring. Then, this fall, you dropped your AP work and are now in Standard Physics, Geometry instead of Algebra II, and a lower-level French. It's still early in the semester so while I don't see anything to confirm this yet, let's assume that this easier schedule will result in continued academic excellence. Yes?"

Enough already. I nod slowly, head down. Say yes, do nothing, and they'll get bored and give up.

"Is everything ok at home, Kat? Normally, we wouldn't pry like this." Bonsky sounds sorry as she puffs her cool minty breath towards me.

"Everything's fine." I pull my sleeves down a little harder as I push the fake smile up from my chest and lift my face. I feel the fresh cuts break open under my tights as I cross my legs. They still don't realize I barely even made it to math class, that I spent most of last period in the bathroom working on my left thigh. Bonsky looks at me sideways, showing an entire row of her perfect white teeth, and blinks once, narrowing her eyes.

"Kat, I think it would be best if we spoke with your parents. Now, don't look at me that way...just a short chat about how you're feeling these days. When's the best time to call?"

I'm fighting with my locker when Amber comes up and pokes me in the ribs. "Where've you been? Elle and I waited for you but then decided to grab some time in the lab. You should see the program. It looks *amazing!*"

Amber has been my best friend since second grade and is the biggest computer geek I know. The girl breathes code. We hooked up with Elle when she transferred into Marshall Middle School in seventh grade and ended up in Computer Systems with Amber and me. I used to have a pretty good time messing around, especially with graphics programs. I even made a site for the Rowing Club last year using pictures I processed myself, but Elle and Amber are so hardcore they make me look like my dad trying to text for the first time.

Amber claims it's a good thing she's so into computers since guys won't look her way, but nobody believes that. A tall slimjim with crazy-thick black hair and skin the color of toasted almonds, she looks like she belongs on a catwalk, not in a computer lab. The only quirk in her pretty face is the funny crinkle that's permanently stuck at the top of her forehead from frowning too hard at math problems and computer screens. She claims this is a hazard of ethical hacking. Elle and I just think she needs to invest in some decent moisturizer.

"The guys in Computer Club are dying to see our code. They were swarming around, asking really idiotic questions about server bandwidth. It was so typical. So, how's the logo coming?" Amber asks, dancing around.

Amber and Elle have been working on an ethical hacking program for NECOM, the Northeastern Computing Competition, and I had been creating a website to house the whole thing, along with a killer logo. This was kind of important since it shows marketability, one of the contest categories. Mr. Rockstad, our Computer Studies teacher and sponsor, said that if we pull this off, we'll go to nationals at the FBI headquarters in Quantico, Virginia. I already know that's not going to happen. Not for me, anyway.

I slam my locker and turn for the front exit. I hope

she doesn't keep asking, but I know she will. Amber's a good friend. She always remembers our plans. If I move fast enough I can get lost in the Friday afternoon crush of bodies swarming out the doors. I don't.

"Come over early, so we can go over the logo before we pick a movie. Oh, and Elle said no feta on the pizza this time but she might be convinced to try pineapple..." I avoid her eyes as her voice trails off. "Kat, what's wrong?"

"I'm...I can't come over. Sorry." I wrap my jean jacket around my waist and look down. I don't want this conversation. Not from my best friend.

"Why not? What's going on? Are you seriously flaking on us *again*?" Amber juts out a hip and crosses her arms. "Look, you've been acting weird since school started. Elle and I are worried about you. First you dump the website for NECOM, which we really needed you to do, then you transfer out of our classes together—literally *no clue* why you would do something crappy like that—and now you won't even hang out. What the hell is going on? My god...did you even *start* the logo? You said you had great ideas..."

She stands straight now, with her hands planted on her hips, confident, assured, mad. I know, in that moment, that Amber doesn't need me. I look up at her smart, beautiful face and feel like an old, flat tire next to her.

"I did, but it sucked. You guys would have seriously hated it." I'm a crappy liar and I know it. I throw my messenger over my shoulder and fly for the exit, avoiding Amber's hurt look, trying not to notice her filling eyes.

"That's it? You're screwing us over again?" she calls

after me as I dodge Adam-the-AV and his rolling cart piled high with laptops. I know I should turn back when I hear her sniffling, but I don't. I walk even faster. Then I bolt...through the doors, across the lot, and past the buses until I have to stop because I can't run and cry at the same time. I'm such a crap friend. Some days, the hurt seems contagious.

THREE

I wake up Saturday morning and, first thing, check out my thigh. Scabs pull my skin too tight. Should make an intriguing scar. I sigh and get up to pee. Paperclips do that. Messy, but they get the job done. Not like those freaks who keep razors in ritual boxes and do all that OCD crap. Totally creepy.

Amber may or may not be speaking to me, Elle will likely be with Amber working on their program, and I'll be doing geometry homework all day, assuming I can figure it out. Today looks like a wash...until I hear the bass. The heavy, thrumming beat echoes up into the bathroom from across the back alley and white picket fence that separates our backyard from the Webers' garage.

I recognize the song, an early single from a 90s grunge band Elle and I both love, something we realized we had in common about three seconds after meeting each other. Even though the whole grunge thing is long dead (my dad actually took us to his favorite band's 30th anniversary tour last year) Elle says it has more grit and life than most of the overproduced stuff radio stations crank out. She made this entire speech in slightly massacred French during an oral final last year, so, while Madame Jolais did look kind of tortured by some of Elle's pronunciations, I could also see she was pleased.

Elle's just like that, a little mouthy but so smart teachers usually let her get away with whatever cause she's promoting. It doesn't hurt that she's small and blonde and most people fall in love with her before they realize how brilliantly sharp she can be.

It feels like a typical Saturday in September, but I don't do shorts or tanks anymore. My mom thinks I'm self-conscious about my thighs. No kidding, but not because I think I'm fat. I put on a long-sleeved black tee and black capris that hit my ankles. Grabbing a banana off the kitchen counter, I head for the back door past my older brother who's at the table shoveling cereal dregs into his mouth. As usual, Pete looks hungover. Normally on a Saturday he'd be at crew practice or working out, but since spraining his lower back over the summer, he just gets wasted a lot.

"Missed a killer keg at Meghan's last night, loser." He squints up into the bright sun pouring through the kitchen window and burps.

"Yeah, bummer." As if I'd party with Meghan the Mac, always sucking on either Pete's face or a cigarette. Pete's a senior at Marshall and he knows exactly how much I detest most of his friends who all pretty much hate me too.

"Oh, wait, that's right, Goth Goddess wasn't invited." He smiles a big cereal-covered grin as I give him the finger and slip through the screen door. I watch a caramel-splotched calico I don't recognize slink around the corner as I stop to listen.

The music, pounding a steady beat, seems to be coming from the Webers' obscenely huge garage, a three-car outbuilding which Mrs. Weber converted to her 'sanctuary' and which Mr. Weber then complained was way too nice to hold the riding mower anymore. I cross the alley and notice smoke coming from a sideways vent in the wall. Weird, because the Webers always go to Florida or somewhere sticky-hot for fall and winter. I'm wondering if I should call somebody when I trip over a big brown-eyed Golden Retriever.

"Chloe, where are you? Chloe?" The frantic voice comes from a girl bolting around the side of the garage. I'm guessing she's left the door open because the music is now totally blaring. She looks both furious and relieved when she spots the dog who has thrown herself at my feet, wiggling uncontrollably. I look down, my stomach knotting as I look into an open, sweet face. I finally reach down and scratch behind fluffy ears.

"Um, is this Chloe?" I ask.

The girl, who's probably in her twenties, shuffles forward in half-laced work boots, shoving firecracker red hair that's fallen out of her ponytail back from her sticky face. "That's her." In our neighborhood of Lily Pulitzer soccer mommies, she definitely stands out in her shredded jeans and paint-splattered tank. I can see some kind of yin-yang tattoo on one shoulder and what looks like a cross between a unicorn and fox high up on her other arm. Despite having on a lot more rips than actual clothes, she's pouring sweat.

I straighten up. "Then Chloe has no pride. One ear scratch and she pledged herself to me." Chloe looks up, wondering if the scratchies are over. Pushing back her hair again, the girl laughs, reaches into a pocket, and pulls out a leash which she clips onto Chloe's collar.

"She's so naughty these days. It reminds me of when she first came home from the shelter last year. We've only been here three weeks and she already knows how to jimmy the door! I'm Tia Lane, by the way, your new neighbor...well, at least 'til next summer when my aunt and uncle get back from Florida. Thanks for finding her."

"Kat Morgan." As she reaches to shake my hand, I'm blown away by her arm. A deep purple scar rips upwards all the way from her fingertips to past her elbow. Definitely not the work of some razor blade. Her hand feels leathery to the touch, nothing like her flawless complexion.

"So, uh..." I am mesmerized by her arm, "the Webers...they're your aunt and uncle..." I've seen some scars, but this is hardcore. Tough and wrinkled, like it was made with the wrong end of a rusty nail. She follows my eyes down to her own puckered skin and busts me.

"Hazards of the trade, I'm afraid," she says, nodding at her arm. "Totally worth the amazing Swedish overlay I cranked out though." My look must have been enough to tip her off to my cluelessness. "That's a kind of glass with different colors that fold down on top of one another. Very pretty stuff. I'm a gaffer." I look at her blankly. "You know, a glassblower?" She mimes blowing a trumpet while twirling her hands.

Got it. Glassmaker. That explains a few things—maybe not the riotous grunge still pouring from the open garage door—but the clothes and, duh, she just said it, the scar. Suddenly, she glances back at the garage and gives Chloe's leash a light tug.

"Sorry, but I gotta bounce. I left the garage turned way up. See you around!" I nod like I know what she's talking about, and say bye. As I walk back through the alley I hear the music mute and figure Tia and Chloe must be inside.

I stop behind the slatted fence to drop my banana peel into the untouched green plastic compost barrel. Another big fat Morgan family joke. So much for Dad's big dream of picking fresh greens and fat vine tomatoes from his backyard. One day he's all about family bonding in the garden and the next, he won't even look at his wife. Funny how things like that happen.

I can see into the kitchen from where I stand. Mom looks tired as she rinses something at the sink, her blond hair falling into her eyes. No sign of Pete...or Dad. I don't know his schedule this week even though Mom still posts his flight times and destinations on the fridge just like she used to when we were little and actually cared.

I hang out on the step for a second, waiting for her to leave the room, and then open the door quietly. Unfortunately, I also crash into a patio umbrella no one bothered to put away. Mom swoops on me as soon as I get inside.

"Kat, we need to talk." She puts down her coffee cup and looks serious.

Crap.

"I know I told you that I'd drive you and the girls to that costume thing downtown..."

"It's a Con, Mom."

"Yes, well the Con then, but the Daleys just called and they need three thousand cupcakes for their rehearsal dinner the same night. I really couldn't say no."

"Really? Three thousand?" Mom's bakery, A Piece of Cake, has been doing pretty well, but the order sounds a little bizarre.

"Ok, more like fifteen dozen," she says, massaging her neck, "more than they'll possibly need, and which I'll then have to pick back up from the restaurant, repackage, and freeze for them, but it's what they want, so..."

"Yeah, whatever. It's fine." I sag a little against the counter. I can calm down now. Bonsky hasn't called and by Monday the principal's office visit will be history. Although Elle and Amber are going to kill me when I tell them they don't have a ride anymore. Amber's mom is terrified of driving in the city, her dad works on Saturdays, and Elle's parents are out of town that weekend which is why we asked Mom in the first place. Maybe we could do the train and then an Uber or bus...actually, screw it. This is better. This way, they know the deal—that they really shouldn't count on me. Not anymore.

Mom looks surprised. "You're not mad? I'm so sorry, Kat, I know I said I'd drive but maybe one of the girls' moms..."

"No big deal." And it isn't. I'm kind of surprised, but I really don't care.

"Alright," Mom shakes her head, "I won't worry about it then. That you'll be fine."

Sure. I'll be fine.

When we found out GamerCon was coming to Philly, we bought tickets as soon as the pre-sale started, and then planned costumes. (I wanted to be Tank Girl but got voted down in favor of us all doing characters together from *Buffy* which, no kidding, is the best show pretty much ever.) Amber knows a guy whose friend's brother even got engaged at a Con, in full costume. People don't care who you are in the real world. Weird gets a pass. Pete and his friends think the whole thing reeks of stupid dork. Whatever. We may be dorky, but nobody I know is dumb enough to pull their lower back showing off in the weight room before crew practice.

I feel oddly light as I go up the steps to my room. My hand feels weird on the banister, like it's not totally connected to my arm. When I open my door, the room looks the same, but I'm behind glass, watching someone else. I'm not upset or stressed or...anything. I'm nothing.

I know we were supposed to do the Con together. But that was before. I don't care about it because I'm not Kat anymore. I don't know what I am.

I feel almost Zen-like as I look around the room at the matching pink comforter and canopy, the off-white curtains and rug, the distressed desk. Who lives here?

Someone takes a bright purple pushpin from the corkboard as a Green Day ticket stub flutters to the carpet.

Someone runs that pin lightly along her arms, across her stomach, over soft blue veins that sit under puckered scars.

Someone slides her capris to her knees, sinks to the soft floor, presses down and pulls, ever so gently, along her inner thigh until the blood streaks and beads, beautiful and ruby, juicy and painful, in a small jagged line.

Again. And again. And again, until the hurt stains my thoughts. I'm here. I'm here. *I'm here I'm here I'm here I'm here.*

I press a tissue on my bloody thigh, jam the pushpin back into the cork, and open *Theories of Geometry*. The total multitasker, I check on my thigh once more as I flip to page 59 where I will try to determine if two isosceles triangles with an angle of 100 degrees are similar or not.

FOUR

Fortunately, the once-quaint Morgan family tradition of brunch—buttery croissants, velvety coffee, actual conversation that does not completely suck—doesn't work anymore, so I do what I want on Sundays. Mom's always out the door before 5:00 AM to get the bakery revved for the post-church rush. If Dad's home, he'll make coffee and maybe scramble some eggs. Then he'll take his food into the den, crank up Sports Central, and Skype with his girlthing. She lives in Denmark or Switzerland or something. I'm not supposed to know about her.

Depending on how hard Pete parties the night before, he'll usually stay crashed in his room until noon. Gary, his manager at the TriplePlex, loves him because he always works the midnight shows. After the shows start, employees can watch whatever movie they want as long as someone stays at the ticket counter. So after Pete lets in his friends, they spike stolen sodas and send whoever else happens to be working—usually pathetic Adam-the-AV or some freshman—to watch the counter while he and his friends catch a movie and get trashed. Pete also makes the loser clock him out long after he's left to party.

Except for Gary, everybody at the TriplePlex knows Pete's deal, but nobody cares. No idiot's going to bust a varsity rower, even if they do get stuck cleaning the bathrooms more than their share.

Something sizzles in a hot pan while Dad hunts in the back of the fridge for his creamer. "Kat!" He glances over, like he's embarrassed I've caught him in his own kitchen.

"Hey." I keep my head down as I dump cereal, milk,

and a bowl on the table. I know he won't be in here long, that we won't make small talk. Suddenly my stomach hurts.

"Sprechen Sie Deutsch?" he asks. I know the answer, but today I don't feel like playing. I haven't for a long time.

"Yeah, Dad, *ja*, whatever." I watch his face fall, watch him push a tiny smile up from his tired mouth. It doesn't reach his eyes.

"Aw, Kat," he starts. This creeps me out because it feels like he might be going for actual conversation. "You doing OK, Kitkat? I know I've been gone a lot lately. In fact, I'm thinking about bidding on an administrative spot in a few months." He sneaks side-eye at me while he pokes at the hot, greasy meat in the pan. "It wouldn't totally ground me, but it would cut air time by about half. I'm always thinking about my Kitkat when I'm up there..."

I shovel cereal I don't taste into my mouth. What a jerk. He can't call me Kitkat. He hasn't called me that since summer. He's barely *seen* me since summer. *You can't pretend everything's fine, that you suddenly like me again.*

"Pink, huh?" He tilts his head sideways to look at my hair. "Will it be blue or purple when I get back next time?"

"Dunno." I scramble for the sink, scrape most of my cereal down the disposal and, even though I'm still in my Hello Kitty PJ bottoms and a long-sleeve tee, head for the door.

"Kat." The tone of his voice makes me stop. "Kat, Mom and I...we know things are a little tough right now."

"Bacon's burning." I point at the curling mess that's begun to smoke. As he turns to reach for the pan, I bolt out the back door. Looking in the window, I see Dad scrape charred bits of bacon and grease into the sink. Mom won't like that. He looks defeated as he grabs his coffee, dumps in way too much creamer, and stomps out.

"Hey, Kat." Tia stands outside the picket fence, Chloe straining at her leash. Somehow, Tia makes the whole ripped-up sweatshirt thing look kind of cool and not stupid retro like when the sophomores in third period French try to rock it.

"Getting ready to do battle or what?" Tia nods at my hand and I realize I'm still holding my cereal spoon. I'm such an ass. I can either slink back inside, embarrassed, or not act like a tool. I walk towards Chloe who wiggles harder than ever.

"Hey," I say to Tia, waving the spoon. "Kind of a long story."

"Yeah," she laughs, "I figured. So, what are you up to?"

"Um, you know, I just kind of ended up out here." I sound like an idiot and I'm shivering. Who ends up outside their back door, half-dressed? "Hiya, Chloe. Are you a good girl today?" She answers by flopping down and giving me her tummy to rub. I realize I should probably say something else so Tia doesn't think I'm some schizoid who walks around the neighborhood in her pajamas with a spoon.

"Chloe and I were just finishing up," Tia says, swinging a bag of dog poo, "and I could use some cocoa. Want some? Unless you have to get back." She gestures at the kitchen where I spy Pete drinking straight from the milk carton before jamming one of Mom's day-old cupcakes into his mouth whole.

"Cocoa, please."

I slide onto a bar stool and look around. The kitchen hasn't changed from the Webers' Memorial Day party a few months ago. Mom always made a fuss about the shiny, unused appliances and the acres of spotless granite countertop, saying she wished her house was that clean. Now small dishes of colored glass, work gloves, grungy newspaper, shiny art catalogs, and chewed-up dog toys completely cover the counter. It doesn't look bad, just like someone actually lives here.

Tia refills Chloe's water bowl and plunks it down before she begins banging around the frosted glass-front cupboards. Mom flips when we slam the kitchen cupboards like that. Tia pulls out some kind of chocolate powder, puts almond milk in a pan on the stove, and grabs a can of whipped cream from the fridge.

"I know, right? Canned whipped cream. How lame. But it's non-dairy. And addictive." Tia shakes the can, pops off the cap, and squirts ribbons into her mouth, smiling. She hands it to me. "Have a go." I shake my head no thanks.

"C'mon, Kat." She slides the can across the counter and, laughing, I reach for it.

"Yes! I knew it!" Tia does a little dance as she turns off the stove and moves the pan. Just then Chloe limps in. Favoring her right front paw, she leans into the counter, whimpering in a way that makes my heart thud. I stop, can halfway to my mouth, laugh frozen in time.

Tia puts the pan down and leans in. "Chloe angel,

what's wrong?" I clench my fists and try to take a breath. "Aw, it's just a little sliver of wood in her pad." I can't breathe. "She probably got it during our walk." I close my eyes. "We can fix that right up, can't we, sweet girl?" Chloe pants and makes happy wiggles as Tia leans in, gently extracting the tiny splinter. I hold my head. Try not to cry. "Look at this, easy-peasy..." Tia stops talking when she looks up. "Kat? You ok?"

"I'm...uh...yeah." Just your neighborhood freak. Nothing to see here. *This is never going to stop.* My head feels swimmy. I shake the whipped cream can back and forth, back and forth until I can breathe again and hope Tia doesn't notice that she has a complete loser sitting on a stool in her kitchen.

Pete scrunches up his face at my pajamas as I step through the back door. "Nice look." I shrug and toss the spoon at the sink, miss, and head for the stairs. "Hey, your dude was at Sumner's party last night. Talked about you too." I swallow hard as I see chewed up scrambled eggs rolling around in Pete's mouth.

"Huh?" Everybody knows Kerry Sumner, a senior on the swim team who tortures underclassmen and whose parents buy beer for anybody who shows up at his obscenely big house. And I know who else Pete's talking about.

"Lawlor was looking for you until I was like, 'Dude, not enough computer lesbians around!'" Pete snorts so hard, he starts to cough. I stand very still. So what if Joey asked about me. I act calm even though my heart rams against my chest when I think about it. He knows I wouldn't be at one of Kerry's parties.

"It was sick! Lawlor totally slammed Sumner at Quarters." Pete turns back to his breakfast, and then catches me off-guard. "I think the dude still likes you or something. He was saying all this stuff but I was like, 'Whoa, I don't want to hear about my sister!' That's just rank."

He still likes me? No way. Not after...everything. Why can't he just leave it all alone? I race up the stairs two at a time, lock my door, and dive into bed. I don't even care when I feel my head smack the headboard. Rolled into yards of pink comforter, head pounding, I wonder if I'll ever stop shaking.

FIVE

I realize somewhere between Lancaster Avenue and Rte. 422 that I've left my phone on my bed, forgot to grab lunch money off the counter, and don't have my French homework. Today already sucks.

As I step off the school bus I see our old green Cherokee parked next to Meghan the Mac's shiny Prius. Pete and I are supposed to share the Jeep but since he has crew practice at 6:00 before class, he gets his own ride and I get the disgusting bus. Even though he's still nursing his back and hasn't actually been to practice for months, he still takes off in the mornings before I can bum a ride. When I complain, Mom says Pete's enjoying "senioritis" and I should let him have some freedom his last year at Marshall. Whatever. Across the lot, Elle and Amber climb out of Betsy, Elle's dented blue Subaru her dad helped her buy last summer.

"Seriously, the bus? Pete ditched you again?" Elle asks as Amber squints at me, her crinkle cutting deeply into her face. She looks like she wants to say something, but doesn't. The three of us fall into step as we go through Marshall's front doors and past Mr. Swenson, the rent-a-cop.

"Yeah," I shrug. "Jackass. Typical." Amber and I head for 6B, our homeroom, while Elle doubles back towards her homeroom in the south hallway.

"See you in the lab." Elle shoots Amber a look and waves goodbye. Amber and I have been in homeroom together since the first day of second grade when she came up to me and asked about my plastic barrette shaped like a huge pencil. Geeks, we joke, spot each other a mile away, even when they're only six years old. As we slide into our seats, she leans in and I brace myself.

"Sooooo, where *were* you all weekend? After you bolted on Friday I really wanted to talk, but you never picked up..." I knew she had called, had seen her caller ID pop up three times on Saturday afternoon as I struggled through geometry. How do you tell someone you were busy, you had homework, you needed to tag your own thigh to not go insane?

Exactly. You don't.

"Yeah, uh, my phone kind of died."

"Your phone died." Amber looks stricken, like I just told her someone ran over Ithaca, her cat. I know that look. She doesn't believe a word I'm spewing.

"Ladies." Mr. McCallister, our homeroom monitor, gives us a warning look and points at the classroom speaker crackling with morning announcements.

...and a big congratulations to the men's eight of Marshall's Rowing Crew with their first place finish in Saturday's Head of the Mason Regatta in Delaware this weekend! Way to go, guys. Student Spirit wants to remind the student body to get their tickets for next month's Harvest Dance. And, finally, Marshall High Mathletes are looking for new members...

Right. The regatta. Joey would have been there. No wonder he was partying so hard at Kerry's Saturday night—no practice on Sunday. What the hell had he said to Pete about me?

Amber pokes me with her pen.

"Are you ok?" she whispers as announcements end. Funny how everyone keeps asking me that. I nod. I'm fine. Couldn't be better.

I sleepwalk through a discussion of vacuum tubes in Physics, a semi-literate debate between two cheerleaders and Traves King, Marshall's All-Star Senior LAXbro, over the definition of "humanness" in Cultural Anthropology, and finally wake up in French as Madame Jolais looks skeptical at my explanation of how I have left my homework, a full page of irregular conjugations, on my desk at home.

"*Bien sur*, Katarine," she says, scrunching her face in a way that would have gotten a student detention. My name sounds pretty coming from her—*Catareeeen*—even when she's kind of miffed. The beauty of the French language or maybe because with her tiny waist and perfect Provence accent, Madame Jolais could, as Elle liked to point out, talk about body functions and still sound hot. As the bell rings and we start to bolt, Madame calls me over.

"Kat?" I turn and find her looking confused. "I don't mean to pry." For maybe the first time ever, Madame Jolais looks flustered. "I know you've got your reasons for changing your course schedule, but I'm still unclear on why you chose *this* class. Wouldn't you rather be in Conversational French with the other juniors? You've missed some assignments but I'm sure you could catch up. I know Elle misses you."

Between Elle's crazy pronunciations thanks to a leftover Houston accent she never completely lost and writing articles *en Français* for the school's foreign language newsletter, last year's Advanced French had actually been a fun class. Elle and I had promised each other that this year's Conversational French would be even better. Madame hesitates.

"You know, Kat, it's ok to look...to actually *be* smarter than some of the boys in this school." So that's where she's taking this. Not bad, but not my deal. Not even close.

Our first day back to school, I went to Mrs. Caine in the front office and changed all the classes I shared with Elle and Amber. Fortunately, I could do it without totally screwing up my transcript. Computer Camp and family vacations had kept them both busy and out of town the second half of the summer so we hadn't really been able to hang out or talk, and when school started my time was finally up. I realized that if I kept even a few classes with either of them, things would crash fast. They both flipped when they saw my new class schedule, so I blamed it all on shitty PSAT scores (not true), my parents being hyper about the SATs (kind of true), and not knowing where my head is (totally true).

But more than that, I knew I needed to be alone this year. I suspected it as the summer drew to a close and I knew it for sure on the first day of school, watching Joey and Taylor snicker with Pete and a bunch of crew seniors in the parking lot. Granted, the logic seems a little hazy now that I'm stuck conjugating irregular verbs with brain-dead sophomores.

"Hey, baaaaaaby!" Taylor screeches as he and Joey swagger down the hall to 4th period.

"Yo, Kat, how's that lab report?" Joey yells. "Taking care of it?" If only I could have gotten out of chemistry too. Stupid. I'm stupid. I turn back to Madame and shrug.

"I like this class, Madame," I begin, but she's already shaking her head.

"Yes, of course you do." She looks sad as she turns

away.

I know things are really screwed when, ten seconds later, I step into Free Study and Bonsky intercepts me before I can even dump my messenger on the table. Even though they should be at lunch or in the computer lab, Amber and Elle wave at me frantically from a table in the back.

"Kat, dear," Bonsky puffs at me, "can you come with me please?" I look back at Amber, who is mouthing something.

"Uh, I have Amber's notes and she needs them." I point back at Amber and Bonsky nods.

"Go ahead, but be brief." I grab a random notebook from my bag and skid between tables.

"What are you guys doing in here?" I whisper at Amber and Elle.

"Your mom's here!" Amber says through clenched teeth.

"My *mom*?"

"She came into lab and wanted to talk to Elle and me..."

"Kat." Bonsky is at my elbow, steering me towards the door. "You can get on the Facebook with the girls later. We've got a meeting right now." She turns to the Free Study monitor, Coach Leonard.

"Mr. Leonard, Kat Morgan will be coming with me," she says with a sharp nod, like a little bird pecking grains. Leonard looks up from the game that's kicking his ass on his tablet, shrugs, and grunts. You'd have to set yourself on fire to get Lame Leonard's attention. We get halfway down the north corridor before I find my voice.

"Mrs. Bonsky, what's going on? Why is my mom

here?" I wonder if something has happened to Dad, if his plane has slid into the ocean somewhere. Until I see my mom's face. She sits in one of the hard plastic chairs in front of Bonsky's desk, rifling in her purse for gum. Students are supposed to drop by the advising office for help with career planning but based on a) the hideously uncomfortable chairs made to keep visits short and b) Bonsky's complete and utter cluelessness, she probably hasn't had many takers in the last decade.

Mom sees me and looks down as I walk into the office. Bonsky shuts the door and gestures at the other chair. *Shit.* I guess Bonsky made that call after all...

"Kat, please have a seat," Bonsky says. Mom takes a shaky breath. Bonsky starts talking and I watch my mom's face turn from princess pink, to fiery red, to sickly yellow, back to pink as Bonsky describes what Miss Clarick has seen of my arms. All we need is pukey green to complete the rainbow. Bad. This is bad.

"Kat, please." They're looking at me. I know what they want. And I hate them. I push myself far away into the corner of the room, float up near the ceiling, stay somewhere safe as I watch a girl in black jeans and orange Chucks cross her arms and sit silently. I want to scream. Instead I laugh.

"Kat, we are trying to help you. *What have you done?*" My mother looks like she might puke. If only she knew. I turn my face to the late morning light beating in through dust motes. Not happening. And no way am I dropping trou in Bonsky's office either, so they don't know about my thighs. Or my stomach...

I've seen worse. Much worse. Like on the Bod-Mod-Xtreme forum where BlondieB in Maryland carves her boyfriend's initials in different places on her body with a screwdriver and then posts jpegs. Now *that's* sick.

Bonsky starts talking again, asking questions I'm not answering while my mom gets more and more frantic and starts yelling. I can't hear her words over the electrical current buzzing in my head. My pulse beats so hard and fast, I almost miss Bonsky's advice, something about looking on the bright side. Fortunately, I choke down my laugh. Mom looks furious. I sit, arms pinned to my sides, mouth shut. I try not to cry. *I'm not showing them anything.*

This is my life. Right now. Right this second. So wrecked I wish I could box it up and hand it to the one person who started all this, who shattered me. Then again, I'm pretty sure he'd just open the box and laugh.

SIX

I start seeing Dr. Caleno on Wednesday after 7th period. Since Pete has the Jeep, Mom picks me up. Nervous doesn't really work for me, so my cuticles are shredded by the time I hit the car. Hyperventilating should be happening right about now until I realize I don't have to say anything to this lady if I don't want to and, total bonus, it gets me out of Mom's Wednesday night meatloaf. Pete can enjoy that all on his own.

Mom looks straight ahead, pretending that she has to concentrate very hard on navigating traffic even though we're practically the only car on the road.

"I think you'll like Dr. Caleno. She comes highly recommended. Mrs. Bonsky said that when another student was struggling with her grades, this woman helped."

I try not to snort. *Grades?* Please. Everybody knows Hunter nailed Raven Connelly for hosting some bizarro food-will-kill you anorexia blog on school servers and she not only had to take it down but also see this school-approved shrink. I highly doubt Doctor Whatever wastes time asking Raven about her GPA.

I notice Mom's hands holding the steering wheel very tightly and that her nails, bitten and bruised-looking, have a funny yellow tinge. I recognize the color; that's exactly how Meghan's hands look, and she sucks down two packs a day in the lot next to the dumpsters. Looks like I'm not the only one with secrets.

Mom lets out a tiny sigh as she turns left onto Carlisle Pike. We pass Young's Bowl-n-Skate on the south end of town where all of Marshall's stoners hang out on Friday nights, and I wonder if Elle and Amber will ever talk to me again. I haven't said anything to them since Bonsky yanked me out of Free Study. Elle stopped texting after Mom used my phone to message her on Monday afternoon, right from Bonsky's office, letting her know I had lost my phone privileges.

My friends don't suck or anything. Amber tried to talk in homeroom, and Elle practically knocked me down at class change in the north corridor yesterday, but I don't have anything to *say*. Well, except that my dad still hates me since Green Day and, by the way, my best friends should start checking train schedules unless they're planning on walking to GamerCon.

Mom makes a sharp right onto Vault Street, and even though I don't completely remember the road, I recognize the houses. We drove past them a long time ago, back during freshman year when we used to go for drives after Sunday brunch, when Dad liked us and smiled once in a while.

Dr. Caleno's office surprises me, mostly because I'm not used to big purple Victorians with blue trim in the middle of a Philly suburb. It hides inside a forest of leaning trees with tiny curlicue leaves. Mom drives over a little stone bridge and pulls up under a huge weeping willow that drips branches all over the car. Even though it's fall, butterflies still flit over wildflowers that blanket the front yard. The place feels like a whisper. I can't even hear the cars I know are zooming down the Blue Route only a few blocks away. We walk up steps to a wraparound porch where a little sign on the door says "Please come in."

"Well, isn't this quaint," Mom says, holding her purse

for dear life and turning the old-fashioned crystal knob. I'm not stupid. I know that's code for, *This is going to knock us back into yesterday.* Mom and Dad's fights about money are no secret. Most recently I've gotten to hear about Pete's college fund, the bakery, and the house mortgage, but only when they weren't duking it out over Dad's girlthing. Always a treat.

We step into a cool blue foyer filled with a huge wooden staircase that looms on the left. Afternoon sun streaks into the hall from behind a stained glass panel, breaking the whole room into colored fragments. A grandfather clock chimes somewhere deep in the house as a sleek tuxedo cat comes barreling down the steps. It skids around the corner and disappears down the hallway, mewing loudly. I remember the lie I told Hunter and Bonsky last week about my imaginary kitten scratching me—*crap*, I wonder if Bonsky told Mom that part—when a voice, cool and smooth like stone, comes from somewhere on my right and makes me jump.

"Please, come in." We step through a short hallway and head for the voice. We look around the enormous room and, for the first time that day, Mom and I look at each other. Then her mouth falls open.

Brilliant blue walls reach up to a second-story loft filled with thousands of books, and then continue up to a huge round skylight that lets in soft, frosted light. The rest of the ceiling pours down stars and constellations painted in gold, like a picture out of a history book. Plants and potted flowers fill the place, including a window seat that looks out into a field of grazing horses. Two entire walls hold CDs from floor to ceiling behind a polished black push-ladder mounted on a track. I almost lose it when I spy a vintage Theatre of Magic pinball machine, dark and sleeping, on its own little island of a rug by a back wall.

Deep within the room, behind a desk made from an enormous cross-section of tree long enough to be a lunch table, sits a pretty girl with curly reddish-brown hair, killer red lipstick, and too many earrings. I'd be dead if I came home with that many hoops. I hear Mom suck in her breath.

"Please, sit." Dr. Caleno comes around to shake our hands. I immediately notice the bright orange capris, but when Dad mentions her later, I'll remember soft hazel eyes. Somewhere out of the corner of my eye, something moves. Another cat, this one fat with creamy colors, yawns and stretches under a potted plant with drippy leaves that almost hide her. I peek around and notice two more cats, one small and stripey brown with a heart-shaped face sleeping under an overstuffed reading chair and another with gorgeous brown, black, and caramel splotches sitting by the window, eyeing me wickedly. Damn, how many cats does this freakshow own?

"So," Caleno smiles, opening a folder and tilting her head so that her short curls fall to one side, "Katherine."

Mom looks confused. "Doctor...Caleno?" I almost start laughing. I can see Mom doing the math, trying not to shit herself as she stares at this girl who looks ten minutes out of grad school.

Dr. Caleno smiles. "Yes, but please call me Lily. I have some questions for Katherine that..." I tune out and fixate on the CD wall. She must have a few thousand CDs. Impressive, although how much crap-pop might be stuffed in there is anybody's guess.

"I'm not a big pop fan but it took an eternity to get the collection together so there might be a few surprises. Anyway, help yourself. Choose some background music." I start when I realize she's talking to me. I look at Mom, shrug, and head to the walls. I've got Florence and The Machine in my hands when I hear the door snick softly and notice that Mom has left.

Dr. Caleno is at my elbow. "We've got plenty of time to talk together as a family, but for now, I'd like to speak to you, Katherine. How does that sound?" I stuff the CD back in the wall and head for the squishy couch in front of her desk. She sits in a chair across from me and stares until my skin prickles.

"Quite a catastrophe, huh?" she says, smiling. I swallow the lump in my throat.

"What?" I feel myself stammer, and it sucks. I'm not going to cry. I don't even know this lady. I'm not showing her my arms. I'm not showing her anything.

"When parents seem like they're going to split. It always feels like such a catastrophe."

I shrug. She pops up and starts walking around the room with a watering can, parting plants gently, tipping the can here and there, talking over her shoulder. "Families can be tough. Sometimes people think it's a shame we can't pick them, the way we choose friends, but families are ours for a reason." I watch her stroll around the room, rambling. I wonder what Mom will say when I tell her Baby Shrink thinks it's important that we can pick our friends blah, blah, blah. I wonder what Raven has to sit through when she comes here. Probably something about how we're all beautiful inside, no matter what we look like. This chick is so into her psychobabble and her plants, I doubt she'd even notice if I go back to the monster walls of CDs.

"You know, Katherine, when you stop cutting yourself and re-channel those impulses, you're going to feel all kinds of things. Confusion, sadness, maybe even anger...at least at first. And it isn't so awful once you know how to handle it."

What the hell? What does she know? My lungs feel funny and my head hurts. I am so ready to go home. I run my hand through my hair, yawn, pick at my totally shredded cuticles. Anything but deal with this wacko. Her next words make me bolt.

"You're safe here."

I stand up and turn around. I forget what I'm looking for, what I'm doing here, so I sit back down. I'm not safe. *I'm never safe.* I jam my hands into my pockets. Pull my hoodie tighter around me. Cross my legs. Try not to barf. This lady knows *nothing.*

"Katherine." Dr. Caleno glides over and sits next to me. "We can do this, you and I." She's nodding hopefully. "Do you want to give it a try?"

As if. I want to tell her to piss off, to leave me alone, to go away. I want to tell her that I hate this, all of it. How Elle and Amber can't know, ever, because they will hate me for being a terrible person, a lame friend, a liar who did things she never should have done, and I will have no one.

I want to tell her because I can't hold it anymore. I want to tell her how I'm tired and scared, how little scratches used to feel good but now, no matter how big or deep I cut, nothing feels good. Nothing feels right. *Nothing works.* I want to tell her so much. But I can't. So

I tell her what I can.

I tell her the only thing I have left.

"Katherine is my grandmother," I whisper. "My name is Kat."

SEVEN

I close my eyes and chew slowly, listening to all the sounds of 5th period lunch, wishing I could disappear. Elle eyes her bologna on white bread in total disgust while Amber stabs at her yogurt. Noise picks up as the lunchroom fills. The Stoners lay around their table, half-baked and happy, handing around some kind of gooey energy bars that everybody knows are loaded. The Jocks make random comments about everyone, and the Straight Edges look bored. In fact, pretty much everyone looks bored except maybe the Student Spirit Squad—aka, Spirit Sluts—Marshall High's perfect and perky cheerleaders, oohing and aahing over a catalog of trashy dresses for the Harvest Dance.

Three new cheer cadets bounce into the lunch line with their stretchy tees. When one of them accidentally bumps Adam Plonski, the poor guy looks like he's been tased. He seems completely lost without his cart of laptops.

"Liftoff!" yells Kerry Sumner, standing by the bottled water machine. "AV's got a boner!" The cadets start shrieking as Adam bolts for the door with his backpack in front of him, looking sick. Torturing Adam just never gets old for Kerry.

Today's special, taco salad surprise, smells especially rank, but that doesn't stop Taylor and Joey from muscling their way in front of an underclassman with nasty acne and popping out the other end of the line with six towering taco shells between them.

"I'm so sick of Joey and Taylor. Like anybody cares they can row," I say. Amber and Elle turn to me with wide eyes.

"Kat, everybody *does* care. Just like you used to." Elle spits out the last part, and throws down her sandwich. The tension sucks all the air from our table.

Amber wrinkles her nose. "My god, that sandwich looks like an autopsy. Please stop trying to wipe bologna juice off everything and go buy a salad." She digs in her bag and comes up with a five which Elle waves off. "Somebody ought to give your mom the memo you went vegetarian, like, last spring." I can tell Amber is trying to help, to make this all not suck so hard.

I nearly turned around and hit the library when I saw them at lunch, at the table we shared last year, the same table we were supposed to share this year until I massacred my schedule. Normally, they'd both be in Rockstad's lab at 5th period, working on their ethical hacking. Not today.

"Kat," Amber sighs, turning back to me, "seriously, we have to talk." She puts down her yogurt quietly and blinks back tears.

"No." I give her a bear hug. "No crying. Not here. You want Monroe sending you to Hunter?" Right at that moment, Marcy Monroe, lunch monitor extraordinaire sporting pants and matching jacket in a magnificent shade of Pepto pink, shoots us a glare as she walks by. The last time Monroe sent someone to Hunter's office, the kid puked on Hunter's shoes. We all look at each other and laugh.

Elle rubs her eyes with both hands. Her smile fades fast. She looks really tired.

"Look, Kat, what's going on? Your mom said the craziest things to us. She wanted to know if we...if we were helping you *cut yourself up* and then she was like, 'Are you doing it with her?' and Amber and I have no clue what she's talking about, and she's super mad, and then Bonsky comes in and drags us to Free Study. What the hell?"

I consider my options: I could crawl under the table, but then I'd have to deal with disgusting floor crud. I could leave but, judging by their faces, that will lose me the two best friends I have ever had. Or, I could do the right thing.

Well, my version of it anyway.

I unhook my left thumb from the bottom of my green surf tee. With deliberate slowness, I lift my sleeve about two inches and turn my arm so they can see three tiny parallel lines of ugly puckered scars that end in a tiny gnarled crisscross at my wrist. *August. Cuticle scissors.* My veins look inky under the cafeteria lights.

They look down, and then look back up with wide eyes.

"Look, you guys, please don't freak out. And don't be mad." They both look puzzled. "Please, it's *ok*. Clarick saw this and told Bonsky, who told Hunter, and then they called my mom. It's so dumb." Elle comes around the table to fold me into a hug while Amber reaches for my hand.

"Oh, Kat..." Elle breathes into my hair.

"And, ok don't tell anybody, but I'm seeing a shrink. I'm pretty sure it's the same lady Raven Connelly sees."

Amber pulls back in horror. "You're anorexic too?" I look at her and start laughing while Elle taps Amber's shoulder and shakes her head.

"Amber, honey, no." Elle smirks while Amber figures

things out.

"Ok, I'm sorry, it's just a lot to process...maybe I should go hang with them," she laughs, pointing at the Spirit Sluts.

"With *that* bag?" Elle points at Amber's beaten up laptop bag, covered in computer logo patches. "Not likely." Monroe comes by and barks a five-minute warning. I carefully hook my thumb back into my tee and grab my messenger while Elle and Amber clean up their trash. So far, so good.

"Kat," Elle asks carefully, "why?"

"What?"

"Why? Why did you do that? And your mom, wow, she's really freaked out. She made it sound like your arms were trashed or something. Not that this isn't serious..."

I look at my best friends, two of the coolest, most pulled-together girls I know. My cheese sandwich, the three bites I actually ate, tries to claw its way back up my throat. I swallow hard.

"Look, it's just..." Elle and Amber sit riveted, ignoring the flow of bodies around us that pour out of the caf and into the hallway, regular kids with families who don't turn them inside out, kids headed back into their words of geometry and physics, English and history. Kids with simpler stories than mine. I sigh.

"It's not a big deal. You guys know how my mom is hella freaked about everything because of the bakery. I told her and Bonsky it was...a sort of accident-experiment. You know, like how you tried pot with Todd the Lifeguard that summer?"

Elle shushes me with her hands. "Kat, shut *up*."

"No, I'm just saying, it's the same exact thing."

"Well," Amber hangs her head, drags an elastic through her hair, and pops back up in a ponytail, "it's not *really* the same, Kat. I mean, you cut yourself. But I guess I get what you're saying. Kind of."

"I don't. What do you mean 'accident-experiment?'" Elle narrows her eyes and hangs her head the same way she does when puzzling out one of Madame Jolais' rapid-fire French sayings.

"Well, I..." Amber and Elle wait for me to speak. How do I say it? I haven't even puzzled it all out myself, just that I need *something*. I want to get inside and find something real, something besides the crap and the lies. *I want to feel.* The blood—the way it beads, turns scarlety-pink where it dots my body—the blood lets me know it's real. Let's me know This Is Me. A wave of hot-cold rushes up from my feet and I'm glad to be sitting down.

"Ladies, get going!" Monroe barks. Thankfully, Elle and Amber gather their things. *This is not for them to know.*

They link arms with me like we used to as silly 8th graders—me in the middle, protected and safe. They walk me to chemistry, not caring they will get late slips for being on the wrong side of the building when the bell rings. They deliver me to chem lab like parents putting their kid on the bus for the first time. My head swoons.

In the back of the lab I see Joey turn on a Bunsen burner until the flame dances up into a high spike. Taylor laughs so hard he falls off his stool while Shelley looks away in disgust. Clarick sees me at the doorway and squares her shoulders.

"Nice of you to join us, Miss Morgan," she sniffs.

Amber holds my arm gingerly, barely touching the place where a tiny taste of hate maps my body. She and Elle whisper, ask if I'm ok, if I'll do it again, if I've shown the shrink. *Nonono. I won't do it again. Yesyesyes. She knows. The secret is out. No need to rinse and repeat. I feel better already. I love you too. No more accident-experiments. Gotta go. We'll hang out later.*

They nod, give me hugs. The bell rings. They run down the hall.

I almost believe every word I say.

EIGHT

I hear a bark just as I'm reading about Alice and Michel's bon voyage to the mall where they have gone to buy *très jolie* shoes. Outside my window I spot Tia by the fence tugging a stubborn Chloe into the alley to do her business. My French book slides onto the floor, bumping my geometry book. I think about crawling back under the covers. I don't.

"Hey, Kat, what's up?" Tia waves as the kitchen door slams behind me. I head for a wiggling Chloe.

I shrug. "Nothing, really."

"You home sick?" Tia stuffs Chloe's leash into her mouth so she can push her straggling hair back into a messy ponytail.

"No, school in-service day. Here, let me." I take Chloe's leash from Tia's teeth. "We can do a loop back behind the park if you want."

Tia, Chloe, and I walk slowly down the small alley until we come out next to Trader's Park. We walk in silence, letting Chloe wander long on her leash, not saying much.

"Tia, what's the coolest thing you've ever made from glass?" The scar on her arm looks especially red and puckered, standing out against the grey sky when she flexes her hand to push a curl behind her ear.

"The coolest thing? I don't know. I guess something I haven't made yet. In my world, the next piece is always the best one waiting to happen."

"What do you mean?" I watch Chloe sniff at the faded benches under the picnic pavilion.

"You never know what glass wants to be, what it

holds. Kind of like how Michelangelo used to say that the marble would tell him what to set free. It sounds hokey but the glass tells me what it wants to be, and then I help it transform. The glass decides." I digest this while a brown and white kitty paw darts out from the benches and swats Chloe across the nose. "What's your favorite subject, Kat?"

"Um, maybe French. Or chemistry."

"Seriously?"

"Yeah," I laugh and start to blush.

"Hey, a well-rounded girl, I totally respect that. Ok, so when you're doing a chemistry experiment, think about that point of no return, the spot in time when the chemical reaction *has* to go forward, when it leaves your control completely." I shudder, even though it's kind of warm, and only a little cloudy. I know about points of no return.

"Yeah, ok."

"Well, that moment, that space in time...that's when the glass decides..."

"What to be," I finish. Tia turns to me and her eyes, a clear green I hadn't quite noticed before, light up.

"Exactly. Come on," Tia says as she gives Chloe's leash a gentle tug. I turn to go and notice kitty eyes under the bench, following, watching.

The heat from the furnace tries to push me back but I plant my feet. The scratches on my safety glasses make everything look swimmy, like I'm watching a show through aquarium glass. Tia yanks me behind a thin metal rectangle on wheels, and suddenly I can breathe again.

"Not so close to the furnace, Kat! We're running at 2400. Stay behind the shield." Before I can say anything, Tia puts on canvas gloves that go to her elbow and begins shoveling white sand into the red-hot furnace hole where it starts to blister and melt.

The Webers' once-pristine garage is completely unrecognizable. The walls of the space where Mr. Weber used to park his riding mower and sneak a beer are plastered with corrugated aluminum almost all the way up to the ceiling except for where three huge speakers hang at odd angles, blaring music.

Between the three zillion degree furnace spread against the back wall, another smaller furnace tucked into the corner, a box on stilts that looks like a portable oven which Tia calls a "garage," and an oversized wooden chair with iron arms, Mrs. Weber wouldn't recognize the place. Tia moves around her workspace like she's spent her whole life here.

"Come look at this," she mouths over the music, motioning for me to take off the goggles as she points to a pile of razor-sharp glass slices that cover a metal table in the middle of the room. The colors look like rainbow confetti. I wonder, just for a second, what one of those pieces—maybe the blue one shaped like a drunken rhomboid—might feel like against my skin. I lean against the table, reach out to touch the glass, and feel the table roll away beneath my weight.

"Watch it!" Tia yells, as the entire table rolls away hard, right into the blistering furnace door. The table wobbles and shimmies from the impact and the shapes slide off and shower the floor in shards. I hold my breath, but Tia smiles and shrugs as she reaches over to the receiver and turns down the music.

"Don't look so terrified. These were extras for something I wanted to try. It's a glass studio, Kat, stuff's going to get broken." I let out my breath. Tia checks on the mountain of what looks like sand she shoveled into the furnace.

"Sand?"

"Kind of. This is batch, a basic combination of sand, limestone and sodium carbonate. Glass at its most basic, before it's actually glass." Tia turns and looks at me with her big green eyes. "Hey, do me a favor, sweep up the shards while I check on something. Broken glass gets really slippery."

After Tia locks the wheels on the renegade metal table, she goes back to poke around in the furnace while I sweep up and then gather the colored bits. A lot of it shattered when it hit the concrete, but I manage to collect a big pile of multi-colored triangles and squares that seem ok. I even find a funky orange triangle. Two inches wide and three inches high, it fits my palm perfectly and reminds me of orange marmalade.

The color burns in my hand like a rusty, juicy sun, except for one random red stripe that runs down the side, like a slow streak of blood. It transfixes me.

Tia has been so cool to me, a total loser freak she doesn't even know. Guilt punches at my stomach as I slip the wicked triangle into the front pocket of my jeans.

"Kat, where have you been?" Mom sounds frustrated. Dad twirls spaghetti on his fork at the head of the table while Mom and Pete sit in their usual seats. No one looks happy, but the gang's all here. Family dinner. Odd but not unheard of. Often painful.

"I was with Tia."

"Tia?" Mom concentrates on stabbing peas with her fork.

"Our neighbor. The Webers' niece? She's a glassblower." I ignore Pete's snort.

"You should have left a note. We started without you." I nod, although no one is looking at me.

"Your father's home tonight." *Duh, he's sitting right there.* I look at Dad and he forces a smile.

"Hi, Kitkat." I hadn't noticed before, but my dad looks old. Old and kind of worn out. The happy bubble I felt in Tia's studio deflates.

"So why'd they cancel your flight?" Pete asks. Dad looks squirmy.

"Engine issues. They'll reschedule in the morning but I gave the shift to Gary. He's been wanting to get there." Dad bites into his garlic bread. I consider bolting, but that'll create its own mess, so I grab a plate, sit, and push around food I don't want.

"Amsterdam," my mother hisses. "Gary and your father both enjoy transatlantics to *Amsterdam*. That's where the cancelled flight was headed." I don't point out that no one asked where the flight was headed, just fight my gag reflex as the iced tea I sipped in Tia's kitchen tries to come back up all over the dinner table. Amsterdam! So *that's* where Dad's girlthing lives. I knew it was one of those Nordic places full of weed and hot blondes.

"Meghan said when her aunt went to Amsterdam she got stoned, like, every day." Pete laughs like a clueless idiot.

"Your father keeps busy in the Netherlands, but not

because he's getting stoned."

"Dammit, Margaret, give it a rest!" Dad shoves back his chair, takes his plate to the sink and drops it, silverware and all, so that it hits the metal with a sharp clatter that makes me jump. Mom seethes as Dad stomps out to the den.

Under the table I reach for the sharp, bright orange point in my pocket. I feel its slick beauty between my fingers. Then I press it to my thumb pad until I feel the gentlest pop.

NINE

"Kat?" Buried under piles of comforter, I roll over and rub my eyes. The clock glows 9:48. Ear buds dig into my cheek as I reach around, feeling for my phone. What the hell does Pete want? My stomach flips as I wonder for the millionth time who he partied with last night, what they might have said about me.

"Kat?" Insistent. Deeper. Not Pete at all. My door opens a crack and Dad pokes his head in. "You up?" Crap. I push myself up and snatch my arms back in under the comforter that rests on my bent knees, pinned by my chin.

"Um...sure."

Dad takes one careful step in the room, like he might hit quicksand. "Hey," he says hopefully, looking unsure, "I was wondering if you'd like to, you know, maybe have breakfast or, ah, do something today." *Do something?*You mean, like we used to...a million years ago?

"Uh..." I rub my eyes, careful to keep my sleeves pulled down.

"Kitkat." Dad moves a bunch of clothes onto my desk so he can sit in the chair. He looks around like he's never been in my room before, then stares at his hands. "I'd like to talk..."

I can hardly breathe. He didn't say much the other night when Mom told him about being called in by Bonsky. About what she saw.

About what I do.

I had heard them mumbling and whispering when I cracked my door. They talked for a while in the den before Mom came upstairs and told me we'd be seeing

Dr. Caleno. I don't know what else they talked about and I don't really care. For once, they weren't screaming about money or Dad's girlthing.

"Dad, um, I need to..." I gesture at the door, hoping he'll take the hint.

"Of course." He jumps and goes to the door, unsure of what to do next. I head for the bathroom. Once inside, I let out my breath. What the hell am I supposed to do? What's he want to hear, anyway? *I like to play with sharp things. Welcome to my world, Dad.* This could not be much weirder.

Pete's door is closed and Dad has disappeared. I stand at the top of the steps and smell the beginnings of bacon and coffee. Sighing, I head downstairs. This is going to suck.

"Hey! How about a cuppa?" Dad throws open a cupboard, grabs a huge mug, and lunges for the coffee pot when he sees me. "Cream, no sugar, madam." He hands me the mug with a flourish and moves back to the stove. The last time Dad handed me coffee was the night of the concert. He called me some things, but "madam" was not one of them and he definitely wasn't smiling. "Hope you're in the mood for omelettes, because this one's going to be killer. I considered soft-boiled, but then I remembered you have a thing with runny goo. Hey, remember that time in the Poconos when you said to the waiter, 'I'm sorry but I can't eat runny goo'? You were ten, I think. The whole place was laughing..."

Dad's babbling in his fast, nervous voice—the one he uses with Mom when the girlthing comes up—and he's swinging around the spatula like he's conducting an opera. The counter overflows with chopped onion, tomato, and mushrooms. A batter bowl with at least a half dozen whipped eggs sits by a sizzling frying pan.

He doesn't see how completely bizarre this all feels. All that stuff we used to do—hanging at the airport, listening in on air traffic, even that one time we went out to the runway to watch a plane park—that's all done. Gone. I wish he would just stop and leave me out of his let's-make-it-all-better project.

I have to get out of here.

"Have a seat, Kat. Keep me company while I cook." Dad leans over the island to push out one of the barstools. I sip my coffee—a decaf Ethiopian organic blend Mom says is stupid-expensive and always complains about buying—and watch Dad chop another tomato. I have no clue how to escape.

I should just go. Say I have a hair appointment, homework to do at Elle's, whatever. I don't want to be here. I put down my mug, push back my stool, look up and see my dad bending over the stove, flipping the omelette carefully, a big smile on his face while he hums Zeppelin. Badly.

I'm still so pissed at him. I don't know how I feel.

If I left right now, he would totally deserve it.

I stay.

Dad plunks down a half grapefruit, a plate of vegetarian bacon, and the largest omelette I have ever seen. Cheese oozes from its center and melts into the brown edges.

"C'mon! Now this is a masterpiece!" Dad sings as he pulls up a stool beside me with his own overflowing plate.

I take a few bites. We eat silently. It's weird as hell.

"Kat, your mom told me about the scratches..." I choke on a piece of bacon, mostly from surprise. "How the one teacher said they looked pretty bad, that you had maybe hurt yourself on purpose."

I poke the cheesy egg congealing into fat yellow wrinkles on my plate and think about how my skin puckers when I pull it at just the right angle. With just the right pressure so the blood bubbles slowly. I put down my fork and swallow hard.

Dad sighs. Shoves some eggs into his mouth. Swings his head towards me. Is he...oh my god, is he waiting for *me* to fix this weirdness? Like I know what to say? *Sorry I like to slice myself up. I can see how your girlthing is cooler than us.* Seriously? It happened the first time I heard him tell Mom he felt lost, that he wanted somebody else, somebody not-Mom. I had heard them fight before. That part wasn't new, but something felt very different. So when I heard the crunch and looked down, I freaked. I had knelt on Joey's CD that cracked in half, leaving a wicked edge. My ripped knee gushed blood and I was scared, for sure, but something else happened too. Not *good*, exactly, but maybe relief?

Let me be clear: crying in the dark in my closet, holding Pink Bear, wanting them to stop screaming and needing to fix the blistered words, I *accidentally* sliced open my knee. It's not my fault I happened to love every disgusting second of it. The fear and pain burned off so fast, I felt wired and cooled down all at once. I felt amazing. And when I tried it again later, with a pushpin, it felt...good.

And no, I'm not sorry.

He should be, though. They all should. I start to push

away my plate as Pete stumbles in, bleary and unshaven.

"I smell bacon." I see Dad wince slightly, then slide from his stool and go to the stove. No more Dr. Phil today.

"Have a seat, Pete. Plenty here."

"Where's Mom?" Mouth stuffed with toast, Pete sprays crumbs across the island.

"Bakery." Dad fills a clean plate with most of his own uneaten omelette and more toast, and slides it across the counter. "Here you go, eat up." Pete hunkers in next to me and starts shoveling food. I see Dad peek at me out of the corner of his eye as he wipes up the stove. I know he's sad. What am I supposed to do about it? I didn't break this family.

What total crap that Dad gets to decide when we're ok, when he'll talk to me, when I'm forgiven. I don't know if he's still mad about the concert, and I'm not going to ask. My body feels scratchy with the memory, like skin twisting inside out.

"So, Dad, thanks for breakfast." I force the words. My stomach clenches.

"Aw, Kitkat, stay and finish..." He knows this round is over. I push away, finally.

"I'm good. But, um, I have a lot of homework so I'll take this." I grab my mug and three slices of Fakin It Bacon. If I can just escape before...

"Hey, Jeremy Rider said he saw Mom at school talking to Braindead Bonsky. What was *that* about?"

"Jeremy Rider's an idiot."

"What, did you ditch or something?"

"I didn't ditch."

"There's hope for you yet..."

"I didn't ditch. Drop it."

"So what *did* the Goth Goddess do?"

"I said drop—"

"Kids," Dad holds up his hands, "enough. Pete, leave her alone and eat your breakfast." He turns to the kitchen doorway. "Kat..."

But I'm long gone.

TEN

I'm so busy fiddling with the headphones and bumping up the bass on the receiver, I scream when she taps my shoulder. And there goes the jewel case, skittering across the hardwood floor, sliding under one of her zillion plant stands. I hate these appointments. Three seconds ago she's on the phone, gesturing for me to get comfortable, enjoy the CDs, whatever. Now she's scaring the crap out of me.

"Kat, I'm so sorry! I didn't mean to startle you." Dr. Caleno looks like she's trying to stifle a smirk. It makes me want to smack her. She finds the bright green jewel case and looks it over. "Oh, 311! Love their sound, all that dreamy stuff mixed in with metal guitar. They remind me of No Doubt...they might be a little before your time though."

Despite the amazing CD collection spanning her walls and the fact that 311 kills, that her headphones cost more than a small car and her receiver alone puts my entire stereo to shame, I want to tell her to stop trying so hard, that there's nothing as gross as an adult trying to act cool. Even if it doesn't really seem like she's acting. Or trying. Still, it's unnerving.

"I like No Doubt," I say quietly.

I snap off the receiver, hang up the headphones, and turn around to find her snugged in her seat, wearing the same expression. I skip the sofa this time and walk to an overstuffed chair as far away from her as possible, falling backwards into it. The cushions swallow me and for a second I feel like a kid who needs a booster seat.

"Sooooo..." I say, bouncing my heels against the

floor. Caleno just smiles, shifts in her seat, shrugs a little.

"How are you today, Kat?"

I rev up for the perfect answer and then remember the plan. What the hell am I doing? I need to focus on getting out of here and away from this lady. Being a jerk won't help. I consider moving closer to her desk to gain 'good patient' points but she beats me to it, getting up to wander the room. She ends up back at one of her amazing CD walls, running her hand over the thousands of jewel cases, pulling one at random.

"Eminem. Great attitude. I always appreciate musicians who can poke fun at themselves. You like his stuff?" She spins towards me and, as much as I hate to admit it, she looks pretty cool. Today she's more casual in leggings, bright pink Ugg-type boots, and a waffle hoodie. She catches me ogling her. "Vegan," she says, lifting a boot my way and turning it so I can see. "Knockoffs. No animals harmed and I couldn't resist the color..."

She slides the CD back into its slot and quietly glides around the room, dusting plant leaves, checking stems, waiting for something.

"I'm glad you found your way here ok today. I know your mom was a little worried about that, but I told her I thought you'd be fine."

I shrug. I drove across town. Not exactly brain surgery. And that explains why Mom let me have the car without monstrous bitching. I would have reported that news flash to Amber and Elle, if they weren't uber-pissed about the website and were actually talking to me.

"Yeah, it was fine." I try to smile but it comes out feeling gruesome. Caleno still moves around the room, touching things in a funny way, like she hasn't seen them before. Or super-likes them and wants to make sure they're really there. She finally ends up back at her chair, looks around, and sits. Weird chick.

"So. Is there something you want to start with?" I have no clue what to say. "We know why Mr. Hunter, Mrs. Bonsky, your mom, and your dad think you need to be here," she says, ticking off their names on her fingers, "but what do you think? Any reason you might want to be here?"

"This is so stupid." The words just pop out, and they're not what a model patient would say.

"Yeah," she nods, "I know it feels that way, having someone in your business. I get it." I decide to give the Good Girl approach a shot.

"I just, um, don't think I need to be here. But," I take a big breath and think about accepting my Emmy, "if everyone thinks it's a good idea, then I'm sure it is. I probably should talk some things out." I'm warming up now. "I know Mrs. Bonsky means well, and Principal Hunter is just doing his job. My parents really do care, it's just that they're busy and working on getting their own lives together and..." I stop. This time Caleno is definitely smirking.

"What?" It comes out sharper than intended.

"Not a thing. It sounds like you have an amazing support system, Kat. Teachers who care, parents who love you. And I bet your brother is equally awesome?" I snort so hard it hurts.

"Pete? Yeah, *he's* a charmer..."

"What do you mean?" Caleno looks interested and even though I know I should just shut up, I can't.

"He's just...he's Pete. Varsity rower, jerk friends, gets

wasted a lot, and never catches shit for anything. Ever."

"Really?"

"Yeah. Big brother of the year..."

"So you two don't share many friends?" Caleno fiddles with her jillion earrings and twiddles a pen between her fingers.

"Uh, *no*. We do not."

"Why's that?"

How am I supposed to explain any of this? This woman doesn't know me, doesn't know how screwed my family is. How crappy it all feels. What's she going to say that I don't already know? That I'm sad and upset? Cutting is a bad idea? She's right about one thing—I am tired of having people in my business.

"So, Kat..." Caleno hesitates for a moment. Drops her pen, thinks about picking it up, and then from across the room, looks me dead in the eye. "Tell me about Green Day."

I think I might puke.

"Green Day?" I go for jaded, but instead my voice comes out squeaky and high, like I've been huffing glue or something.

"Yeah. What's up with Green Day?" Before I can even blink she glides back to the enormous CD wall, runs her fingers over a few jewel cases, almost magically pulls out *Insomniac* from the thousands of cases and then starts humming 'Brainstew.'

"You saw them this past summer with Joey Lawlor."

I nod. I can't even talk.

"Your dad said you came home pretty intoxicated."

I stare at a block of color on the Oriental carpet. If I blur my eyes just right, it almost looks like a kite flying through jagged waves. Or a dragon going in for the kill. My fingers itch for something sharp, something wicked. I can't breathe. I kick at the carpet, stop the dragon mid-flight, ruin the kite's lazy wave tumble.

"My dad?" I want to say more, but don't trust my voice. I don't trust anything.

"Your parents and I had a chat before your first session and he kept bringing up the Green Day concert. He thinks you began drinking around that time. I'm sharing this because he said he mentioned all of this to you, that you know how upset that night made him."

Unbelievable.

"Kat, are you okay?" If only I could breathe, or swallow, or think straight...

"I did drink that night. But I don't drink anymore. I mean, I didn't drink that much before, just now I don't drink anything." God, this is insane. "And I'm really sorry. That it worried my dad. It's all fine. I'm...fine."

I make a face that should pass for whatever sorry looks like. Hopefully she'll praise me for my honesty and we'll be done for the day. Caleno leans forward. Looks at me. Smiles. I brace for the thank-you-for-being-a-good-girl speech.

"Kat, I appreciate you speaking with me, because I know this can be awkward." Caleno taps her bright red lips with a blue sparkle polish-covered fingernail. *I've so got this.* "But it might feel better to actually, you know, share the truth sometimes." She shrugs. "Just a thought."

ELEVEN

"Oh…" Amber's voice trails off. I knew she'd be upset.

"Amber, I'm sure you guys can grab a train that gets close to the convention place. We were near there that time we went to that stupid-expensive dress store and they were like, *Ladies, can we help you?* Remember? You'll figure it out." I use my middle fingers to spin the orange triangle's sharp points between my thumbs, gently balanced between one thumb pad and one fat red scab. The triangle's blood-red stripe winks at me through morning sun pouring in my windows. I turn it sideways and rub its flat side up and down my arm until the glass heats up and takes on an odd, almost-slick quality. I love the way it slides over my skin like silk.

"Wait. *What?*" Amber's voice vibrates into my stomach where the phone sits cranked on speaker. I imagine the line on her forehead getting deeper and deeper.

"I know this sucks and I'm so sorry but…"

"No, Kat. Don't even. First your mom can't drive anymore, and now it's 'You guys.' What's *that* supposed to mean? How are *you* getting there?" I wait a beat before saying anything. This felt a little easier when I practiced it, but not much. "Tell me you're actually blowing this off." I'm silent. "Just say it." Tears prick behind my eyes. My two best friends. I am going to lose my two best friends.

"I can't go." I feel no relief once the words are out. Instead, as usual, I feel like I want to puke.

"I don't *believe* you!"

"Amber…" I hear her breathing, think she's maybe

crying. She's definitely pissed.

"Talk to me, Kat. I'm dying to hear this one. Tell me you're going to stay home and maybe, what, clean your room? Wash the Jeep? Have a chat with your dad?" Ouch.

"Amber..."

"This is total crap. We planned Con since the summer! *What is going on?*" I hear her voice change then, as panic settles in. "Wait. Does this have to do with the cuts? Are you grounded or something? Does your mom still think we had something to do with that?"

I take a shaky breath. "No, my mom doesn't think that. I just...I can't go."

"Ok."

I'm scared by what I hear in her voice. Or maybe it's what I don't. I knew this would happen. What did I expect?

"I have homework so..."

"Wait, Amber. You know I'm sorry, right? That I wish I could go?" Suddenly, the light coming through my window is too bright, too white-hot shiny. The lies I tell my best friend split and fester. Terror grabs at me. Amber sighs.

"Bye, Kat."

Come...as you are, as you were, as I want you to be... I knock once but I know there's no way Tia will hear me over the music. I open the Webers' garage door slowly and am blown away by the volume. I see Tia across the room, hands swirling and twirling a long rod with gobs of glassy goo on its end slowly across a metal table. She looks up just as I try to figure out a way to get her attention. She walks the rod, goo and all, to some kind of oven across the room. She closes the little shutter doors on her half-finished piece and heads over, sliding her hand across the receiver's volume knob on the way.

"Hey, Kat, what's up?" If I didn't always feel like such an alien, I would say something cool. But I do, so I don't. I stand there, feeling stupid. Tia has stuff to do, art to make, things to get done. And I'm just in the way, the weirdo neighbor girl.

"What, you can only hang when you're in PJs with your spoon?" Tia bites back a laugh. "Come inside already."

Maybe it's the way she looks at me, like she doesn't want one damn thing from me. Or the pressure that explodes under my ribs when Tia lets Chloe nose her way in from the kitchen, where she zooms across the studio, and flumps down for rubs.

"Ok," I say, right before I burst into tears.

Tia pushes a steaming mug of something that smells faintly like toasted rice to me across a small patio table tucked into the corner of the studio. Even after she swipes at the tabletop with her sleeve, everything, including the two beaten stools, show a paper-thin dusting of batch. She looks at me gently as she blows on her own fragrant mug.

"Things rough at school?"

"My friends are mad. I think they're done with me." I surprise myself when I say that.

"Yeah? Did you do something to piss them off or are they just being jerks?" I shrug, look up, meet the green eyes I can feel drilling into me. Tia pushes up her sleeves, stretches long, and lays her arms on the table. With her left index finger, she traces the deep scar up along her right hand and past her wrist, landing near the crease of her elbow. "Sometimes you have to trust that friends will ultimately understand even if they act like they won't."

"I don't think it works that way."

"Why? What did they do, ditch you? Break a promise?" The guilt twists inside me. Elle and Amber aren't the ones breaking promises.

"Not exactly. I don't know…there's just too much wrong. Too much to fix."

"Says who? Friends trust each other. Without trust…" Tia traces her scar back down her arm, more forcefully. Something in her eyes gets soft. "…things can go really wrong."

I think of Mom and Dad and his girlthing, of Joey, of Pete, of all the people I love and hate at the same time, all the people I trust. Or not. How bogus.

"Trust doesn't work," I blurt.

"Yeah, it can be hard. Lots of good things are hard, Kat. But when it works between people who know what it means, it's great. Your friends might surprise you. Hey, how'd you get that wicked puncture?" Tia stares at my thumb scab, green eyes clouding over. I grab at my cup so hard, I almost tip it.

"I don't know." Subtle.

"Looks nasty." I feel my face turning red and hot, feel Tia staring at me, through me. What would she say if I told her I used one of her glass shapes—one I *stole*—to bust open my thumb? That feeling my blood bubble up like fat drops of rain felt amazing?

"Kat, is this about some guy?" My breath catches.

"Some guy?" I sound stupid.

"Yeah. It seems like it's more than just friend stuff. And in my vast experience," she says, rubbing her face and smearing dust across her chin, "this kind of sad tends to be about a guy." I raise my eyebrows. "Or a girl, whatever. Point is, it's usually about some completely toxic relationship that feels good but just isn't."

"Yeah. Sort of. I guess."

"You guess. You don't know?" I watch Tia stand and stuff her hands into her pockets. *Of course I know.* If she really wants to know the deal, I can show her. And not the stupid way I barely showed Elle and Amber, or the way I refused to show Bonsky and Mom. No. I could just say *screw this* and really show her. Yank my sleeves up to my shoulders and talk about how slicing near the elbow makes a wicked bleed but crappy scar. Lift my shirt and point out straight lines of healed-together skin on flat abs that no one will ever see. Show her puckered and bruised thighs covered in scars that dip and weave around blue-black veins. And then tell her everything. It would feel nice to tell her everything...I could start slow, maybe talk about Joey, see what she thinks.

"Hey, I can use some help in here if you're up for it." She looks at me expectantly, reaching down to retie her boot.

I start breathing again. The moment has passed. She wouldn't know what I'm talking about anyway, just that I'm broken. Then Tia would tell my mom who already knows, kind of, who would then tell Dr. Caleno...gah. Dr. Caleno. What the hell am I going to do about her?

Eye on the prize, like Elle always says when she's conjugating really hard irregular verbs. If I can just get through a few more sessions with Caleno, say the right stuff, she'll cut me loose. Maybe I'll even show her my wrist boo, the same one I showed Elle and Amber. That might be enough to keep her happy and feeling useful. I'll be *very* sorry, act grossed out, maybe look a little surprised and sad. Just enough so she gets the picture. I'll even throw in some sniffly story about Dad's girlthing. Shrinks love that crap.

I've totally got this.

I slurp the last of my tea, snatch up the safety goggles, and wipe my eyes.

"Absolutely. Love to help."

TWELVE

I almost don't ask. But then I do.

"Did you get highlights? They look really good." I whisper the words fast, around morning announcements in homeroom. I need to get her talking because the silent treatment is on my nerves. Even if I do deserve it.

"Yeah. Elle did them." Amber jams a few books into her backpack harder than necessary, just to let me know she's still pissed. No kidding. When a Spirit Slut starts rambling about Harvest Dance tickets on the speaker, I roll my eyes. Amber shrugs, looking down and away.

Just get through today and tomorrow and then I'll have the weekend to do...nothing. Even though I haven't exactly been acting social lately, it still sucks to be alone. Never mind that I created this whole mess.

I spy Elle on my way to physics, rushing through the west hallway towards the older lab where she and Amber slum it on days freshmen swarm the new lab. She doesn't see me, but even if she did, I know she won't have much to say. I don't bother calling her name because how many times can your best friends look at you like that until it starts to really suck?

Just as I crawl into my seat and Ms. Wu cranks up a YouTube video on the secrets of thermodynamics, Hunter gets on the announcement system and starts clearing his throat. Never a good sign.

"Ah, students, this is Mr. Hunter. We'll be, ah, having a mandatory assembly for all students this morning. Please file into the, ah, main auditorium at the bell and we'll proceed from there. Thank you." Wu powers down the laptop and turns off the projector, leaving us to wander to the auditorium. As we gather our junk, I overhear two seniors.

"Yeah, and then I heard Traves King blew some crazy number on the breath thing."

"Breathalyzer?"

"Whatever. He was completely trashed. Can you believe it?"

I don't bother to look for Elle and Amber as we shuffle into the auditorium like cattle. I'll stay for 10 minutes, get a bathroom pass, and head for the library. I just don't have the patience for an assembly today. I notice Bonsky flitting around the edges of the room, dabbing her eyes with a tissue while Principal Hunter talks to a cop in the corner. What the hell? The Spirit Sluts huddle up front by the stage, crying and holding on to each other. Hunter climbs the stage and moves to the mic, clearing his throat nervously. The room quiets to a dull whisper.

"Everyone. Everyone, I need your attention." The cop stands by the side of the stage, looking self-conscious. "Students, we have some news...there's been an accident. A terrible accident and, ah, we want to share what we know so far with you."

Everyone shifts in their seats. Hunter sees Bonsky hovering on the fringes of the room and gestures for her to come onstage. Bonsky winds her way to the front, sniffling and wobbly, while Hunter stands there, sausage fingers opening and closing. The whole thing would be amusing in an afterschool special kind of way if it wasn't quite so unnerving.

I spy Pete in the back with his friends, looking bored.

Just as Bonsky nears the stage someone lets out a ripping scream from the north hallway. The whole room jumps while Hunter and the cop both look towards the door.

Cassidy Falls—senior, Spirit Slut extraordinaire, Traves King's girlfriend—crumples to her knees just inside the door.

"He's dead! I know he's dead!" she scream-sobs. Her posse, which includes every cheerleader in the room plus the entire lacrosse team, rush over to her, knocking chairs out of the way. Hunter, looking pissed at being upstaged, tries to get the room under control.

"People, settle down. Settle down! *I need your attention!*" The cheerleaders drag a sobbing Cassidy to a seat while the lacrosse team circles the girls, unsure what to do.

"We've had a report of an accident that occurred this morning. Around 7:30 AM, four members of Marshall High's sports teams were involved in a car accident at the intersection of Broadway and Franklin. The boys were rushed to Central Hospital. Traves King, the driver, and a teammate remain in guarded condition. The fourth passenger, Kerry Sumner, was pronounced, ah...ah...he died at the scene. Officials have stated that..." but no one is listening anymore. Cassidy, no longer the grieving girlfriend, looks confused, while other kids start crying. I know my cue when I see it.

I head for the doors while Hunter blathers into the mic about "...grief counseling...all-day access...free study..." My stomach flips when I see Pete talking to Joey and Taylor by the main doors. Seeing them all together, wondering what they're saying, always makes me slightly ill.

Everyone looks kind of scrambled and voices inch up to a dull roar in the auditorium as I take the double doors and head for the library. No pass needed today. Good luck getting that mess under control.

Kerry. Bully of the year. Seems like karma. Once last year he tried to have a pizza delivered to detention but didn't realize the guy wouldn't be able to get into a locked high school. Pete thought it was the funniest thing he had ever heard. Elle, Amber, and I voted it dumbest prank ever. And now he's...gone.

Since I have no clue when the bell will ring for 2nd period, or if we'll even have regular classes today, I turn towards the main library doors and push through. Everybody loves Traves, so there will definitely be lots of crying. Maybe they'll even dedicate the next bunch of games to him if he's hurt badly. I don't even know who else was in the car.

I walk through aisles of Books By Dead White Males and American Poetry Nobody Reads until I reach Chemistry Corner, a private spot of ancient books no one has touched in decades where Amber and I used to play games on her tablet, before she and Elle spent all their free time in the computer lab. But I can't sit because, holy crap, *she's* in my seat. Our private, game-playing, no-one-ever-sits-in-this-seat seat.

"Well! Hello, Kat." Caleno tilts her head to the side in a way that reminds me of a cat watching string. You. Are. Shitting. Me.

"Hi...uh...uh..." I sound just like Hunter.

"Oh," Caleno looks around for a second, pats the table. "I'm sorry. This is your table. Let me move my things." I watch her scrabble together some papers with one hand while she mouses windows closed on her laptop with the other. Windows full of...YouTube cat videos? Seriously?

"Um. Hi." Who knew my school was a portal for an alternate universe. "What are you doing here? At school?"

Caleno stops gathering her stuff and shakes her head. "I'm here for student support." She suddenly looks very sad. "Grief counseling, Kat, for your classmates...because of the accident." Oh, right. I nod, look around, pick at my nasty cuticles.

"So this is where you're doing the counseling? All the way back here?" I ask.

"No, Mr. Hunter has a classroom set up for me. I'm just waiting for the assembly to end...which I guess it has since you're here."

"Yeah, I guess. Or mostly anyway. The Spirit Slu...uh, cheerleaders will be looking for you. They seemed pretty upset. And the lacrosse team." I shrug. Lots of people at Marshall like Traves and the lacrosse guys.

"And you? How are you, Kat?"

Ha, *no way* are we starting that. I heft my bag. "I'm fine. I wasn't really friends with those guys, so..."

"Well, if you want your table, it's all yours." I watch as she packs up her papers, grabs a few folders, and shoulders her laptop bag. She's exchanged her zillion hoops for a zillion studs, instead of sparkle blue her nails are now black—for the occasion?—and today's lipstick is a super-charged cherry red. This woman even makes grief look sexy. The lacrosse team will love her.

I stand awkwardly, wondering if I should say something else.

"Have a peaceful day, Kat."

I nod and drop my messenger on the table. When I look back up, thinking I should say something to look at least a little less socially stupid, she's already gone.

75

THIRTEEN

"Gently, Kat. Don't let the piece droop." Sweating into my goggles, I blow hair out of my eyes. I lean onto the rod lightly as I roll the hot glass on the end of the long pole along the metal table to give it a smooth shape and keep it from sagging.

"Good. Now, a tiny bit of air," Tia says. I puff into the tube and, of course, the glass bulges like an insane water balloon.

"Crap!" I press and roll furiously to try and deflate the stupid bubble, but it doesn't work. I've ruined the piece. Tia just laughs.

"I said a *little* air! Ok, let's take a break." Because I'm working with clear glass, Tia dumps my ruined mess back into the main furnace where it will melt again. I feel stupid but at least I haven't wasted her stuff. I take off my goggles and wipe my face. I rub my ashy hands on my jeans and remember just in time to avoid the tops of my thighs where fresh scabs heal over old scars. Again.

At least I can spend Saturday doing something that doesn't suck. Or hurt.

"You're doing great, really getting the hang of it," Tia says, pushing two glasses of iced tea across the dusty patio table. As she bends down to unlatch the half-door so Chloe can slip into the studio from the kitchen, I see a chip of cloudy blue glass around her neck.

"Hey, that's cool," I say, pointing at the slip of blue. "Did you make it?" The pendant is shaped like a guitar pick and layered with multiple shades of solid blue on blue. Tia tugs it over her head and hands it to me.

"Nope. You're looking at ancient art. This is Swedish

Blue, a smelting scrap from about 400 years ago." The small triangle of glass radiates a solid, cool feeling into my hands which feels nice in a room full of furnaces pumping out constant heat.

"Hey, that's the same blue..." I point at three huge swirly-colored vases that sit on a shelf against the front wall. Tia's face pinches and she looks away.

"Not really. It's different." The vases stand really tall, taller than any glass pieces I've ever seen. Because of the way she has them arranged, they almost strike a pose and look like something I once saw in the Philadelphia Museum of Art.

"Ok." Considering I don't know crap about art glass, I just nod and sip my iced tea, wondering if maybe I should go, even though Tia asked me to stay for the whole afternoon to help. Something weird's going on.

Tia sighs, clenches her hands, and gets up.

"Come with me." I look up in surprise, put down my iced tea, and get up. I figure we're going outside, but when I reach for Chloe's leash Tia shakes her head and takes my hand. Her fingers feel like sandpaper on my palm—rough and tired, but very gentle. She leads me to the front wall, to the shelf near the door. And then I see she's about to cry.

Letting go of my hand, Tia hefts down the first vase, a tall piece about four feet high made of pale watery blue glass coated in crazy swirls of darker blue. I almost yank back when she props it on the ground and leans it into my hands. When I realize how phenomenally stupid that would be, I stop and hold my hands steady to receive it. *Don'tletgo don'tletgo don'tletgo...*

"What do you think?" She looks it over with an

artist's eye, seeing things I know I never will. So I tell her the first thing that comes to mind.

"It's beautiful, like two oceans meeting." Tia looks at me and the tears puddle down her face. As fast as she started crying, she stops.

"Sorry. Thanks for that compliment. That's truly a lovely way of describing this. It's called Swedish overlay because of the way the one color comes down and folds over the clear glass. See?" I look closer but can't see the place where the two pieces have swirled and melded. It reminds me of how, once an experiment has begun, it's nearly impossible to pull out individual components anymore.

"One of my glassblowing teammates, Teddy, would always say my pieces came straight from the ocean. I guess I'm just feeling sentimental."

"Your teammate?"

"You need a team for making bigger pieces like this. The little stuff I make now, the wine glasses and some of the art glass, that's totally different. With the big, bold pieces you need someone to blow air, someone to help shape, someone to add color..."

"So how many people made this?" I slide my hands along the cool blue glass.

"This was part of my second series, so even though different people in the studio would jump in and help, there were always at least three of us doing the core work." I hand the vase back, anxious to get it out of my hands.

"It's pretty cool."

"Yeah. I loved this series. I titled it *Outliers*...seven oversized lantern vases that were supposed to exhibit."

Tia stops and closes her eyes, and I feel like I'm getting a bird's-eye view into her life. I have no idea what to say. She smiles.

"You've seen this, right?" she asks, holding up her scarred arm, smiling. I swallow. "I know it's hard to miss, and I appreciate you not being a jerk about it, like the people who point and fake-gag."

If she only knew how I rivet my eyes on that scar every time I see it. I find it awe-inspiring, the way it twists and winds up her arm like a dried, cracked river.

Tia tells me the story I knew was coming, how a friend of her teammate, Julia, splattered liquid glass onto her arm, how it seared her skin until she blacked out from the pain, how the wound ended up so deep, they cancelled her art show that month. And then when it wouldn't heal, they cancelled it for good. I had already guessed most of the story, just without details.

I always knew Tia's scar came from her art. Even if she hadn't casually mentioned it when we first met, you don't have to be brilliant to figure out that a talented glassblower with a magnificently fucked up scar who won't make anything bigger than a wine glass probably had some horrible accident. I kind of wish my story could look like that.

I can't blame my scars on some clumsy stranger or my amazing love of art.

Not that Tia does any of that. Too cool to throw a pity party, she pulls down the two other vases to explain how she got the colors to run or sink into the glass a certain way. Then she smiles like she actually means it and, after having me put on my goggles and go over the safety routine again, starts me working on what will eventually become the ugliest paperweight in history.

Nope, her story can't be mine. Not because I can't dig around and find some blame in others if I tried. Her story can't be mine because I cut because I can't *not* cut. I cut because that's what I do. I don't make art, I make pain.

"Kat?" She's been talking. I'm supposed to be rolling the hot glass she's once again blobbed onto the rod for me. I stare blindly, liquid glass drooping at a crazy angle, right onto the metal table. I try not to cry. Tia takes my mess back to the furnace for the second time. Smiles. Looks me in the eye.

"I'm sorry. I know the whole scar thing is rough, but it's a part of my history. I struggled for so long..." I open my eyes wide. She believes I have a problem with her super bad-ass scar. As if I could ever be as cool as her, with her crazy talent and sweet dog.

Chloe shuffles over, snuffling for treats. When she sees I have none, she presses into my legs and looks at me with big chocolate eyes. It all feels so unfamiliar. When I'm with Tia and Chloe in this hot, sticky studio I actually feel something I haven't had in a while. *I feel safe.*

"I can't..." I start, but my tongue gets stuck.

"You can't what?"

"I can't...I can't do this."

Tia's face looks pained. "I'm sorry. I shouldn't have shared so much. It's a lot to digest."

"No!" I sob, "I mean *me*. I can't do this anymore!" I push up my sleeves and thrust my arms towards her, into the afternoon light. When Tia pushes back her hair and leans in to look, I feel like a saint in those religious paintings, arms raised up, like I'm praying to something I can't see.

Except I'm no saint and I have no clue what faith feels like. And when I see the look twisting Tia's face, I'm pretty sure she agrees.

"What's this about, Kat? What's going on?" Tia stands very still, waiting. I sniffle and look away. I see immediately that this was *really* stupid.

"Talk to me."

"I, um...when I feel bad I..."

"I can see that, Kat," Tia snaps, catching me off guard. "What the hell?"

"I should go." I start putting away my tools, slipping my glassy mess back into the furnace.

"Ok, hold on. Just...wait." Tia rubs her face, a sure sign she's stressed, while twisting her hair out of her eyes into an uncomfortably tight-looking knot. "Come sit for a second," she says, patting the old patio chairs.

"I figured you'd get it," I say lamely, drawing circles in the batch dust on the table.

"Yeah, ok, I get needing to show someone. But do I understand? Not really." We sit in a tense silence, the only sound in the room Chloe snuffling around.

"I'm seeing someone about it," I offer.

"That was my next question," Tia says quietly.

"She's kind of weird, my counselor."

"Yeah? Weird how?" Tia asks, rubbing her own scar.

"I don't know. She always...it's like she knows things."

"That *is* her job." Tia looks like she doesn't know what else to say.

"It's like she's, um, psychic or something."

"Psychic?" Tia looks more than skeptical.

"Yeah. I told you, *weird.*"

"Well, ok. That's...curious."

"Anyway, I should..." I wave my hands vaguely at the door. When she doesn't say anything, I get up to leave.

"Kat?"

"Yeah?" I ask, hand on the door.

"Please get help. And I'm sorry."

I nod and step outside before she can see me crying.

FOURTEEN

I look around and snug my palms around my toasty double-latte. Juliette Denn and Raven Connelly are poking around by the bakery case, picking out $3 cookies they'll sniff, chew for 30 seconds, and spit out. Apparently, their bones aren't jutting enough, although I swear Raven's elbows could take out someone's eye.

Nobody from school comes to Piccollo's. Well, except Elle, Amber, and me on Saturday afternoons last year when we needed somewhere with decent coffee to study. A Piece of Cake was out since Mom wants the tables for paying customers. Kids from Marshall usually hang out at Warm Milk on the other side of Ardmore Avenue, especially on Monday nights because it's all-ages open mic.

There's nothing trendy about this place, a café that serves simple lattes and overpriced cookies, but we like it. For once, maybe the first time since they got really pissed at me, I'm actually glad Elle and Amber aren't with me. I really just need to think...which is why it figures I'm running into people from school I have zero interest in talking to.

"Hey, Kat." Raven cuts her eyes at me as she walks by, swinging a bag of cookies while Juliette licks froth from her cup. I wonder how many calories are in milk pumped with air. She probably knows, so I don't ask.

"Hey." I instinctively pull my sleeves lower.

"So," Juliette says, slurping her drink, "did you hear? The lacrosse team's going to hang a banner for Kerry's memorial and Cassidy The Amazing Girlfriend—*barf*—is making a speech since Traves is still in the hospital. We weren't gonna go but Kerry was always cool about letting me borrow his trig homework so I figured we should. To show respect and stuff. What are the rowers doing for a memorial?"

"Dunno. Pete didn't say." Pete didn't say because I didn't ask, mostly because I don't care. Everyone always thinks I've got dirt on the rowers just because Pete and I inhabit the same house. Like we even talk. I blow on my latte with great concentration and look away, out onto Moss Street. I hope they take the hint.

I notice Raven staring at me, eyes huge in their sockets. The girl seriously needs a sammich. Just knowing she and Juliette do the Chew and Spit gives me the heebs. I consider telling Juliette she looks like a rabid dog the way she darts her tongue in and out of the milky foam, but I feel too worn out to bother being bitchy.

"What do you think of Caleno?" Raven asks, making me choke. I finish coughing before I turn around to really look at her.

"*What?*"

"Caleno. The shrinky-dink. Thoughts?" Raven flips back a chunk of super-straight, jet black hair flat-ironed to perfection—I love it when parents pick grotesquely perfect names for their offspring—and drills her big doll eyes into me. Thanks, Mom. Awesome of you to stay subtle and not spread my business around the whole neighborhood. "Definitely *something* up with her. Haven't figured it out. Yet."

I shrug and turn back to the window, holding my breath until Raven and Juliette eventually wander out. They head down the sidewalk, sharing a cookie. I look away when I see them spit it into a napkin.

Caleno. I still don't know what to think of her. She's around 45 by my guess, way older than she looks until you look really closely, and seems cool enough with her funky clothes and killer CD collection. Ok, and also because she shrinks her patients in a crazy awesome room with stars on the ceiling and more books than Pete could count, but it's not like I really know anything about her.

I watch a pretty calico covered in tan and caramel-colored splotches slink around the corner and sit by a blue hybrid, tail swishing. It almost looks like the cat from the park, the day we were walking Chloe, the first day I ever touched glass in the studio. Actually, Tia would probably like Caleno if she met her.

Part of me regrets shoving my arms up in Tia's face but another part still feels less shredded, like my whole body isn't turned inside out anymore. I guess someone whose own arm looks like it went through a blender tends to be less judgmental than your average jerk. I can see how having an outrageous injury that stopped you from making art would seriously dampen your life. But that's not me. I might have a load of scars, but it's not the same. No one sees them. And I don't need help fixing my life. I make a mess of it just fine by myself.

When the cologne hits me, my stomach drops. Three seconds later I hear the laugh and see the dress blues.

He orders for both of them. For himself, a plain coffee, for her—a pale blonde in a tight blue skirt and dorky print scarf—something frothy. All dressed up except for his uniform hat which he must have left...in the car? In some hotel room? The latte curdles in my stomach.

My dad: smiling, laughing, ordering, paying, carrying. Now sitting two tables over. With some lady. Probably a flight attendant. Hard to miss the uniforms. They sit down close together, half hidden behind a leaning bookcase. *If you kiss, I will puke.*

He leans forward, touches her hand gently, leans back, takes a sip of his coffee. Their intimacy envelopes the room; watching them make out would almost be less gross. Almost.

They laugh, look serious for a minute, talk some more. I always thought Dad's girlthing was safely hidden in some cold, faraway place, not right here in town. He gets up and goes to the counter to pick up a piece of pie and a cookie the barista serves up. He brings them back to the table, smiles, and attacks the pie like the world is a happy place full of warm dessert, not broken daughters who shove things into their skin.

The lady nibbles on the cookie. Looks thoughtful. Probably wonders how to get rid of us, of *me*. She wears dangly glass earrings made of a pale, watery glass that matches her translucent hair and skin. She reminds me of a jellyfish, guts visible to the world but safely tucked away.

I think about the colors that fill Tia's studio, the way the glass garage, the small prep furnace, keeps all those fiery reds and deep ocean blues warm and melty, ready for the next evolution. I've watched Tia work simple tubes of color into killer art glass, taking her time, scorching a color with a blowtorch to help it transform, seeing where it wants to go and then letting it fly.

Nothing stays simple and one-dimensional in Tia's studio. Even her wine glasses have a funky feeling to them, shaped by her crazy energy. Her lantern vases don't tower anymore, but I've watched her put more love into a simple wine glass than most of the posers at Marshall put into an entire semester of art class.

I realize in the moment how much I miss my mom, from before, when she did more than bitch at Dad and worry about her bakery. I guess I miss Dad too. Before he decided we weren't enough and never would be and, worst of all, left us even though he still shows up for dinner and pretends. How did this all spin so far into space?

I'm so sick of it. Tears drip onto my books and my hands shake, making me slosh latte on the table. Still the loser who can't keep her shit together. I feel around in my jeans pocket for the orange triangle and then rummage through my messenger. Where did I leave it?

The woman stands and heads for the bathroom. Although I can't tell since he's half-hidden behind the bookcase, Dad seems to be humming to himself as he polishes off his pie and coffee. I wonder where they'll go after here. To screw somewhere? The thought makes me ill. And then I kind of feel...nothing.

If I could stop crying I'd follow her and say something. It would be weird, but no more than confronting my dad right now while she's off peeing. I wipe my nose and wonder what he would do if I walk right up and ask him to introduce us. Would he just ignore the whole thing? Maybe. Mom basically does.

Shoving my books into my bag, I stand and try not to shake. I bus my table, putting my mug into the grey bin by the trash and dare my father to look at me. To turn and see me standing there, watching him, waiting, hating. Of course, when he does I almost throw up.

"Kat!" he says from his table, standing quickly, coming over to get rid of me before she comes back. But instead of shoving me outside, he just stands there and smiles.

"Hi, Dad," I mumble, not knowing where to look.

"Hey, I'm here with a friend but we're just about done. Can I give you a ride home?"

What the hell is wrong with him? "What? No. I, um, have to go."

He looks confused as I shoulder my bag and sprint for the door. When I hit the sidewalk I see the calico dashing off down the street, making a guy on his bike yank hard to the left to avoid her. I turn back and see Dad motioning to me through the window while the girlthing stands next to him, looking at me like I'm a circus freak. I really want to give her the finger, but instead look away when she waves at me through the steamy glass.

Yeah, keep waving. Whore.

FIFTEEN

The last highest score on Theatre of Magic blinks and I look twice to make sure I'm seeing it right. I didn't even know numbers went that high on pinball machines. I guess whoever played it must have been really good…or really crazy.

"Kat! You found my favorite table." Caleno wanders into the room wearing insanely cool jeans, a scuffed up Calvin Klein tee, and silver bangles stacked to her elbow. A pain in the ass, but she can dress.

"Oh, hey, Dr. Caleno." I decide to at least pretend I'm ok being here since I so want to be done with this crap and not talking isn't going to speed that up. For now, I'm going for civil. "This is pretty cool," I gasp as I come dangerously close to tilting with a hip-check. I started playing while waiting for her to start our appointment. I see the machine every week but I can't exactly say, *hey, shrink yourself for a few* while I play. Amber and I used to rock the pinball machines at Geno's Arcade in Ocean City when we were younger. I could almost forgive Caleno with toys like this.

I land a solid hit on the magic trunk and get ready for my multiball when I spy one of her cats darting across the room. Tan and brownish, it reminds me of the caramelly-colored one from Piccollo's, and the park, and…

"We can get started as soon as you finish up your multiball." Like clockwork, the second she starts talking, I lose three multiballs in a row. Grrrrr.

"I'm done." I take a seat on the couch in front of her today. Not knowing what to say, I arrange my face and stare at my Vans. God. So. Over. This.

"How are things?"

I shrug and, out of habit, pull my hoodie sleeves farther down over my hands. A little voice of dread in my head hopes she won't bring up Green Day again. "Tell me about your week, Kat."

"It's only Wednesday."

"Ok, so tell me about your week since last Wednesday."

"Um, there was a memorial for that lacrosse player yesterday."

"Yes, Jerry." Caleno gets a funny look on her face, like she wants to say more, but holds back. "A lot of students at Marshall are pretty devastated about that."

"Yeah, I guess." Pete and the rowers did some lame tribute in the cafeteria at lunchtime but since I skip lunch for the library most days, I missed it.

"How are things at home?" I look around the room and resist the urge to go rifle the CD wall. Instead I plunge my hands into my hoodie pockets and discover my orange glass point. Using my thumb, I slide it across my right palm and feel its cool slickness. Then I test the point gently against my thumb tip. The scab has healed but there's a scar. Caleno leans forward.

"What do you have there?" she asks.

"Huh?" I drop the triangle and put my hands in my lap. She leans back in her seat. Freak.

"Your dad...he wanted to come to this session, but I told him not yet, still girls only."

I blink hard at her. "*What?*" I try to keep the snark out of my voice. "Why?" The nasty tone slips out anyway. Caleno smiles kindly, like I can trust her. Right.

"He's very upset that you wouldn't speak to him at Piccollo's. I presume you know he headed out," she looks at her watch, "on a 7:00 PM flight last night and will be gone a few days. He's worried about you."

I snort. "Yeah, worried I'll ruin his affair." Caleno tilts her head and plays with her pencil. When she lifts her arm, her zillion bracelets clink.

"Secrets can be rough. Talk to me." She's not smiling anymore.

"Huh?"

"Your dad made mistakes and now he's trying to fix things. I'm not sure it's going as smoothly as he would like, but he's trying."

"By going out on a date? *That's* how he's trying to fix things?" I do it again. I open my mouth and suddenly there's a flood. Resisting the urge to shove the orange triangle through my palm, I blab about the dreamy blond girlthing in the café who should be in Amsterdam and how Dad cornered me in the laundry room a few hours after I saw him, wanting to talk while I shoved towels into the dryer.

"I know. That's why he wanted to come to today's session. To clear some things up," Caleno says. "Kat, that wasn't a date. Margie isn't a girlfriend, she's an old classmate from flight school..."

"I don't need to hear it," I snap, confused. It never occurred to me my dad might have friends like that, but whatever. Still not the point. That's when I tell her about Mom's desperate hatred of all things Dad, about the night last summer when I overheard Dad tell Mom he wanted a different life, careful to leave out the part about the CD and my knee.

"He doesn't want us anymore. He hasn't for a long time."

"Why do you think that?"

"Because he pretty much said it!" I feel queasy and hot. My hands start to itch so badly I dig into my palms with my nails. I unravel. "He hates me."

"Your dad?"

I nod because I'm sniffling. I hate this. Weirdly, I also feel relief—no matter what I say, Caleno can't tell anybody. At least, I don't think she can. I bury my face in my hands and hope I pass out, but that would be too easy.

"Kat," Caleno says way too calmly, "I would like you to hear something." She digs around in a file and pulls out a piece of paper. "'I love Kat's energy, the way she brings light with her when she steps into a room.'" She looks at me. "Not the words of a man who hates you."

"What are you reading?"

"A list of things your dad loves about you. He made this list at my request when you and I started seeing each other."

"Things he *loves*? About *me*? That's just..." I wipe my nose with my sleeve and try to think this out. "It's easy to say nice things when the person isn't right in front of you," I sniffle. Caleno continues reading.

"'I love the way Kat thinks for herself, the way she never lets anyone push her around. She's independent and incredibly smart.'" I feel punched in the stomach. *The way she never lets anyone push her around.* If he only knew. My newest cuts throb. Handiwork from last night. Instead of the tender patch of soft skin where inner arm creases into elbow, I have a series of crusted-over scabs. X marks the spot...

"Ah, so that's it, eh?" Caleno nods at the slice of orange glass I'm holding. My heart leaps.

"Lucky charm," I mumble, shoving it back into my pocket. She smiles and lets it go.

"So, your dad wanting a new life, something different...you feel responsible for that?"

"I don't know." *That's a lie. I do.* Caleno looks at me without blinking. Her hazel eyes swallow me whole and, when I really look, I see flecks of gold and something else, something incredible. I start crying again. And then really stun myself.

"He's mad about the concert. About Green Day."

"About Green Day," Caleno repeats, almost hypnotically, "and..."

"Joey. He's mad about Joey. About the whole night." I can't breathe. My skin tries to turn itself inside out as I sit there feeling raw. And stupid.

So incredibly stupid. I want to go back. I want it all to go away.

Caleno comes around the desk and sits next to me on the couch, just like she did at our first appointment only a few weeks ago. She takes my hand gently, like she's afraid I might bite or throw up on her.

"What happened to make him so mad?"

"I came home sort of...drunk. He was just, you know, kind of upset," I lie. He was way more than upset.

"So he was upset because you were drunk?"

"I don't know." I lie some more. The dad who used to let me look around the cockpit? Who convinced Mom to let me dye my hair green? Who took me to get second holes in my ears? Yeah, I'd say he was "upset." Caleno looks at me—through me—and suddenly I'm opening my mouth, starting to speak, until I catch myself. I snap my mouth shut and she almost looks...guilty.

"So you come home drunk, your dad is mad, and that's it?" she shrugs.

"Yeah. He made me drink coffee. He yelled at me. I went to bed," I say. Caleno moves slowly back to her desk where she sits and starts tapping the tip of her pen.

"Kat, what about that night makes you cut?"

"What?" I ask, shoving gum into my mouth. Get me out of here.

I'm suddenly sweating, pinned under her look, a glare so sharp it reminds me of the sharks at the aquarium. Her usually soft hazel eyes have gone flat black. For a second, I don't even know where I am.

"What's with the nasty?" she asks, too casually, pointing at my thigh as she gets ups to hand me a bottle of water she's pulled from somewhere under her massive desk.

I freeze. What the hell is going on? I look down, expecting to see the words I carved into my thigh—FUCK ME—bleeding through my jeans even though it's a couple of days old and scabbed over. I look back at her and see the air around her shimmering a swirly pink, like blood mixed with rain.

Somehow, my mouth opens and I speak. "I got mad," I say, breathless. "I got mad and that's what happened."

She nods. "Yeah, I figured. That's not exactly a love letter to yourself."

I pick at the frayed knee of my jeans. What am I supposed to say to that?

"So is that what happens when you think about that

night? You carve nasty things into yourself?"

I nod.

"Kat, we're out of time for today but this has been productive. We're headed in the right direction." I stand, find the door, and go.

As I zombie-walk to the car, trying to figure out what the hell just happened, I glance back to see small diamond-shaped cat eyes watching me before they disappear behind a fluttering green curtain.

I'm so out of here. I skid onto the main road and floor it.

SIXTEEN

I fall into my desk chair and laugh. How utterly pathetic.

Who *wouldn't* laugh at that hot mess, Paula Conte, Senior Spirit Slut, giggling like an idiot while Joey jammed her up against the lockers, covering her entire mouth with his tongue. Only Mr. Starkinski's superb timing, and not wanting to see grinding against his classroom door, stopped them from doing it right there. When homeroom bell rang they scuttled off like roaches caught in the light.

"Hey, are you ok?" I turn to find Amber looking at me. So now we're talking?

"It speaks!" I joke, which is exactly the wrong thing to say. Amber eyes me in a way I'm not sure I've ever seen.

"Forget I asked." She half-turns away and starts digging in her bag.

"I'm sorry. Amber, I'm sorry. For everything." I shut up when announcements come on and fiddle with my old-but-new thumb scab. Blah blah, Harvest Dance tickets, blah blah, get well card for Traves King in the front office, blah blah, Kerry Sumner Memorial Fund…I tune it out. Amber shoves a crumpled paper at me as the bell rings and she bolts for the computer lab.

"Here. In case you actually care. You used to." I open my mouth but, when I can't think of anything to say, I close it and watch her go.

In classic good timing, Alberta Phun, Marshall High's LGBTQ President, announces through the tide of people pouring out the door that she'll be petitioning to allow non-binary and same-sex couples on the Harvest Dance King and Queen ballot, something Hunter already nixed. Marshall High mommies and daddies can be as open-minded as the next parent, but let's not push things. McCallister packs up his laptop and shakes his head. Good luck with that, Al.

While Ms. Wu continues a chapter on boundary behaviors in physics, I pull out Amber's paper. The email, from some official-sounding dork place, announces the top fifteen NECOM entries. Amber and Elle's names sit third on the list, under the Marshall High logo.

So they're really doing it. I remember Amber bouncing into English lit last spring, stage whispering how she and Elle were the first girls at Marshall to ever have scored a spot in NECOM. When Mrs. Victoria, tired of the distraction, asked her to share her news with the whole class since it was obviously more important than our discussion of *Frankenstein*, Amber actually stood up and made her announcement, huge smile plastered on her face.

That day at lunch, Amber kept shaking her head while Elle squealed, both of them claiming there was no way they could have the program ready in time and more psyched than I'd ever seen them.

I remember being excited to mash up a website for their data. When I wasn't doodling logo ideas I'd cheer them on, fetch lattes and cookies when they got stuck, and slather Amber with moisturizer in homeroom those mornings after she had been up all night. And now they finished it, their big thing...without me. My choice, but still. I'm happy for them but so sad.

"Kat? *Kat?* Hello, Kat. Are you with us?" Ms. Wu, the

perkiest physics teacher ever, stands looking at me. Some of the class has turned around. In Geekville, people actually expect you to know answers. I like physics and last year I would have killed this class. But now I'm having a good day when I get my name right.

"I'm sorry, Ms. Wu..." I shake my head. She's not letting me off though.

"Ok, let me repeat then: upon reaching the boundary, a portion of the incident pulse will be reflected and, thusly, remain in the same medium. A portion of the incident pulse will also pass into the other medium...which lies where?"

I crunch the email in my hand and feel scabs yank as I flex my arm. It hurts. Everything—my friends, my schoolwork, my whole fucking life—has turned into an enormous mess since the summer. I see my father's red face as I stumble in past curfew, Green Day songs and screeching tires rolling around in my head, his veins pushing against his neck as he screams. "You have no boundaries, Kat! Always pushing, even when you have no idea what's best for you! And *you*," turning to Mom, "always letting her get her way. Just like with this concert. Kids need boundaries!" That was about the time I heard Joey's tires squealing away down the street. Sure, Dad, boundaries. *That's* the problem. I sigh.

Ms. Wu clears her throat, waiting for me.

"The other medium lies...beyond the boundary," I say.

"Very nice, Kat." Ms. Wu nods and turns to the board. Sometimes my life is such a joke.

"Kat, dear." Bonsky intercepts me in the hallway

between Madame Jolais' classroom and study hall.

"Hi, Mrs. Bonsky." I put on my best smile, which makes me look like I need to pee.

"A moment in my office?" Asking what she wants won't help. It never does with teachers like Bonsky, so I just follow. Joey and Paula walk by, Taylor following behind looking pissed. Even though seeing Joey always makes my stomach twist, and seeing him with Paula makes me kind of squeamy, seeing Taylor look miserable almost makes it worth it.

"A seat," Bonsky says, gesturing to the horrible plastic chairs. I haven't been in here since the big meeting. I drop my messenger at my feet and wait.

"So." Bonsky looks at me expectantly. "I know that when students, especially those who are generally very high-achieving sometimes strike a rough patch in life, they tend to shut down a little, sometimes even withdraw..."

I tune out and notice the plaques scattered along the wall behind her desk. Bonsky has every stupid platitude covered. "Kindness Matters" and "Follow Your Dreams" and, my favorite, "You Can Do Anything!" hang at quirky angles behind her. When I hear the name, I'm yanked back.

"...from your mother that you have been seeing Dr. Lily Caleno." Bonsky smiles and raises her eyebrows. I nod. "And this has been going well?" I nod again. Sure. Great. It's been going great. "Kat," Bonsky shakes her head, "I need your assistance in assessing if things are going well with the doctor. If the, ahem, *situation* is improving..."

"It is!" I smile and nod. Crap crap crap. I should have

been ready for this. Bonsky lights up.

"Yes? Things are better?" My neck feels like it might snap I'm nodding so hard. "And the doctor, she did the usual tests during your initial visit?" I know Bonsky's talking about the suicide questions. At my first appointment Dr. Caleno had asked a bunch of questions about hurting myself. When I finished answering she told me she didn't believe I was trying to kill myself—duh—but that she had to ask, just because.

"Yes. Dr. Caleno is...great. It's helpful to talk to her." I try not to smirk as I say this but then realize it's not a complete lie. I'm still puzzling this out as Bonsky makes notes in my file, humming to herself.

"Have you had any family sessions yet?"

"Uh, no. So far just me and Dr. Caleno. Except for the first appointment. My mom talked a little to Dr. Caleno after I was done, but that's it."

"No family session?"

"No." I shrug.

"That seems unusual," Bonsky says, puzzled, "and irregular."

"No, it's not," I assure her. "Not with a family like mine. Family therapy will come later. There's plenty of time." It sounds so formal, I almost laugh when I parrot Dr. Caleno's words from my first appointment. I'm also surprised at how totally annoyed I feel by Bonsky's suggestion that Dr. Caleno isn't doing her job right.

"Well, Kat, this does seem like an improvement. I'm sure Principal Hunter will be relieved."

"Is that all, Mrs. Bonsky?" I gather my bag and stand. Ten minutes of sitting quietly with this woman feels like I've run a marathon.

"Yes, Kat, thank you. Here's your hall pass. Take care!" As Bonsky waves me away, I eye the cheap wooden plaque stuck to her door that reads "Guidance" and wonder if anyone, at any time, has left her office feeling guided, ever.

SEVENTEEN

I get off the bus with a ripping headache, barely noticing Mom's car in the drive. Joey nearly got us kicked out of chemistry when he and Taylor lit a book of matches on fire. Clarick, of course, bought his excuses about how it was an accident, but not before she almost gave us all detention. Shelley was like *I have Mathletes* which was a dead lie and Taylor and Joey claimed they had weight training for crew. Clarick just looked at me, waiting for my after-school activity excuse. When I didn't answer, she told us to "straighten up" and went back to the podium.

I pour some iced tea and hold the glass to my head. The red low-charge light on the phone cradle in the kitchen blinks slowly. As I head to the stairs, I hear mumbling and see Mom in the den, hand to her head, phone jammed into her shoulder.

"...not sure. Bob and I are ridiculously busy, so I think it's something she did for attention." Mom waits a second and then says, "Yes, it certainly did work. The counselor says that's not it, but why else would she do that? It makes no sense, Lucy. The one chemistry teacher, she said her arms were sliced up like...like...*lunchmeat* or something." My hand, slick on the glass, slips. Mom. Gossiping with Aunt Lucy. About me.

A full glass of tea smashes onto the hardwood.

"Kat? Pete? Hello?"

I grab a dustpan from the kitchen and clean up as fast as I can while Mom wanders into the hallway as she says her goodbyes to Aunt Lucy. I ignore the wet smears along the floor left by my sloppy cleanup and bolt up the steps to my room, slamming the door. Digging the orange triangle out of my sock drawer, I curl my fist around it as I fall into bed and crawl under my comforter, jeans and all.

"Kat?" Mom calls from outside my door. "I'm coming in, honey." She cracks the door, tiptoes inside. I hear her take a big breath. "I'm here now, so you don't need to do anything. You don't need to...to hurt yourself. You have my full attention. I am fully present. Right here, right now."

I roll over and look at my mom through a tangle of hair. "Why are you talking to me like I'm retarded?" Mom looks as though I've slapped her.

"We don't use that word in this house, Kat." I already know this. We don't say "retarded" ever since my cousin Andrew was hit riding his bike and ended up with a brain injury. Which is totally not the point, and she knows it.

"Right, Mom. Got it." I roll tighter in my comforter.

"So you heard me talking to Aunt Lucy." Obviously. Then she pulls out the same sugar-sticky voice she likes to use with Dad when she wants something. "Kat, *please*." It creeps me out enough that I roll over and face her.

"What the hell, Mom! Why would you talk to Aunt Lucy about this? You think I'm desperate for attention? Seriously?" I'm so mad, I'm panting. How she puts together ambushing me in Bonsky's office and forcing me into therapy with begging for attention, I cannot fathom.

"Yes, I was talking to Aunt Lucy. She loves you and I needed to talk to someone. This is so confusing for us. For your dad and me. We don't know what we did wrong, only that you're hurting yourself..."

"Mom, please stop." I try to roll away and face the wall.

"That blog said girls who do this crave attention, and we've been so busy..."

"You're reading a blog?" Despite myself, I'm kind of impressed. Mom barely even uses the computer. Amber and I built A Piece of Cake's website and Mom's baking assistant, Patty, checks email. Just using her cell pushes the bounds of her techno savvy. She sits on the edge of the bed, twisting her hands into the comforter.

"Yes. I've been reading about...self-injury. It's scary stuff." She whispers this last bit and looks like she's going to cry. "I thought at first maybe Amber and Elle were doing it too..."

"*Mom.*"

"I did. I thought you all did it together, like a *thing*. The three of you were so close." She looks so sad. "Honey, why don't Amber and Elle come over anymore?" I can't believe she even noticed. I shrug.

"They're busy."

Mom sits back. "But what about you? I thought you were helping with that computer program thing and now, nothing. The only time you ever go out is across the alley to see the Webers' niece."

"So? She's nice." Mom knows I hang out with Tia? I wonder what else she knows. I grip the triangle a little more tightly, being careful not to slice open my palm. "Can we please just not talk about this anymore?" Mom's eyes well up.

"How are your sessions with Dr. Caleno? Do you think they're helping? Do you two talk about things?" This makes me sit all the way up. I'm stunned. Dr. Caleno actually kept her word. She said she'd only share information with Mom and Dad if she felt it was an emergency.

"Yeah, it's ok. We talk. Why are you home today and not at the bakery?"

"I was at the bakery." Mom looks dazed, her eyes bright and glassy. "I just decided I needed a break so I came home early. I left Patty to close up."

And that's when it slips out.

"Are you and Dad getting divorced?" Mom jumps up and starts gathering clothes scattered around my room.

"My god, Kat, who told you that?"

"No one. I just wondered…"

"Things are really confusing right now," she says as she folds a concert tee hanging across my hamper. "Your father and I need to figure things out. The bakery needs to do a little better if we're going to keep the lease on the building and Pete has to decide what he's doing about school next year, if he's going to Community or what…" she trails off, like she's lost her train of thought.

"That's dirty." I point at the shirt. She nods and places it, perfectly folded, into the hamper. I see tears in her eyes again. Looking at my clothes strewn around the room seems to overwhelm her. She pushes a stack of CDs and old French homework out of the way and plunks down at my desk, looking more tired than I've ever seen her.

"We're working on things, Kat. Your dad and I. And we've been so…just so worried over you." I want to be mad at that, but somehow I'm not. It just makes me sad. She folds a pair of dirty gym socks into a tight square and places them gently on the edge of the desk.

"Honey, I have to ask you this." Mom stops fiddling with my dirty clothes and looks at me. "Why do you do it?"

I knew she would ask eventually. I'm surprised she hasn't yet, but now that the moment has arrived, I'm speechless.

"Mom..." I swallow and my throat makes a dry click, like a bomb about to go off.

"The blog said that girls seek attention and that alcohol use increases the risk. And after the whole incident with the concert..." Hands tucked far inside the comforter, I squeeze harder and feel the edges of the triangle begin to slide into my palm. "I even took some notes. I know you probably think that's dumb, but I'm just trying to understand."

My heart jumps into my throat. She took notes? The same woman who drives me completely insane, always bitching about the bakery's bills and Dad's overseas flights, *took notes*. I look at her, curled into herself like a kid in my oversized desk chair, fiddling with my dirty socks. My throat clicks again and I wish I had my iced tea.

"That's not dumb, Mom." I'm glad I don't need my French printouts because, even though Mom has covered her face with her hands, tears drip through her fingers and onto my desk while her shoulders shake. I've never seen my mom cry before, except the night Dad announced he wanted a new life.

She reaches for a band I use to wrap my hair and I don't say anything when she wipes her nose with it. She looks startled when she realizes what she's done.

"Peer pressure," she sniffles.

"What, Mom?"

"The blog says peer pressure can be a factor. Who's pressuring you, Kat? I need to know so I can help." I sneak my hand from under the comforter and take a peek. My palm shows a triangle imprint delicately edged in blood. I put the triangle on my bedside table, tuck my hand back under the comforter, and look at my mother crying at my desk.

"The blog is wrong. It isn't like that."

She doesn't look convinced. "What do you mean?"

"I don't know."

Sniffling, she looks at me, unbelieving. "I want to understand this. Why won't you talk to me?"

"Mom, I *am* talking to you. And I'm trying to explain that I don't like it when you talk about this with other people, especially Aunt Lucy."

"Kat, this isn't about—"

"Mom, stop talking to people about my business. Let me figure this out. That's what Dr. Caleno is for, right?" Even that one surprises me.

"Yes, that's what's she's for, but it doesn't mean we can't be upset and worried."

"Well, then you'll be worried no matter what I say anyway. When I figure it out, I'll let you know." It comes out sounding bitchier than I meant it to, but Mom takes the hint. She moves to the door, looking defeated.

"I don't know what to say, Kat."

I shrug. "Neither do I."

EIGHTEEN

"Did you show her?" Tia asks as she nudges the mini-furnace doors closed with her elbow. She brings over a bright cerulean blue hot dog of glass, specially imported from Germany, and attaches the molten glob to the bottom of the vase at the end of my blow pipe.

"Um..." When Tia texted to ask if I wanted to help with a piece of Swedish overlay, I said sure. Plus, I really needed to see if she was still kind of freaked out or whatever.

Even though the vase is only half the size of the ones on the front wall, its weight makes my arms quiver. The bright blue glass, soft and pliable, begins its slow liquid fold over the vase. I swap places with Tia. She takes the blow pipe from me and begins spinning the glass over a wad of newspaper folded like a huge pot holder that I hold flat in my gloved hands.

I wet the pile of paper with a squeeze bottle between rolls so that when the hot glass meets it, small puffs of steam go up. We work in silence for almost 30 minutes until, eventually, the colored glass folds down completely over the outside of the clear vase, coating it in a bright waterfall of color.

"You *didn't* show her." She sounds mad. I knew she would. Tia takes the vase still attached to the blow pipe and walks it back to the mini-furnace where it'll stay warm and workable. I drop the soggy newspaper, pull off my gloves and goggles, and wipe my face. Here it comes. "You said you were seeing her to get help."

"I know. I *am*. We just got kind of sidetracked..."

"Your shrink got sidetracked? Kat, you showed me

your arms but you didn't show...what's her name?"

"Caleno."

"You didn't show Dr. Caleno. Why even go to a doctor if you're not going to ask for help?" Tia stands in the middle of the studio, crazy red hair springing out of her ponytail like a wild halo.

"She's not technically a shrink." Tia doesn't move. "What I mean is, she's a doctor, but not a psychiatrist. Regular shrinks only give out pills. Dr. Caleno is actually a psychologist."

"Your *arms*, Kat. You failed to show her your arms, the entire purpose of seeing this doctor, because..." She makes a twirly, get-on-with-it motion with her hands.

"We talked about other things," I whine. "And she already basically knows about my arms." Tia raises her eyebrows in a question, but mostly looks unimpressed. Not surprising since she's heard me whine about a zillion times already and I've only known her, like, two months. "Seriously. We did. We talked. I swear. And she *does* know."

"Look," she says, softening, "I know this is rough, but you have to take care of yourself. And that means talking to the people who can help you. The only reason I didn't march you back home and talk to your mom last week is because you said you were seeing this doctor." I don't say anything, just take the can of orange fizzy water Tia hands me out of the tiny studio fridge.

"My mom knows." I regret it as soon as it comes out.

"Not the point!" Tia practically yells, sending a curious Chloe scurrying away from the studio half-door back into the recesses of the kitchen. "You showed me some serious shit and said you were getting help." Tia lifts a shaky can of seltzer to her mouth. She looks like she might cry.

I tend to have that effect on people.

"I'm not equipped for this, Kat. I just...make art."

"Please." I slump on the batch-powdered patio chairs, hoping Chloe will come back to the door and ask to be let in. Any diversion would help right now. "I know I have to show Dr. Caleno. I just can't. Not yet."

"Don't you trust her?" Tia pushes back a clump of sweaty hair with her magnificently scarred hand. This makes me snort. How ironic.

"No, she's actually kind of cool. I trust her well enough. You'd like her."

"Yeah? Then what is it? Besides the fact that no one ever wants to talk about painful stuff."

"Just...if I tell her..."

"Tell her? But she already knows about the cutting. Isn't that the point of seeing her?"

I cringe a little. "Yeah, she *knows*. But if she actually sees it, she's going to, you know, want me to stop." Tia's head snaps up and her green eyes drill into me.

"Of course she's going to want you to stop. But she's there to help you learn how." I start to sniffle, a sure sign I'm going to bawl.

"I can't." The tears well up.

"You can. And she *will* help, Kat. It's not like she's going to drop dead in shock when she sees your arms. If she's in this business, she's seen worse."

"But I can't stop."

"Yes, you can."

"No, I can't."

"Yes. You *can*. With help."

"No, I can't."

"Look, once you—"

"*I don't want to stop.*"

Tia looks down. Sighs. Pulls out her ponytail elastic and runs her hands through her hair, making it huge. Then she sits down across from me in her usual spot, rolling her cold can of water between smudgy hands. "Fair enough." I look up in surprise at her words, wiping my eyes on my sleeve.

"When my arm got mangled, I didn't know what would help me feel better. I don't mean the pain meds, they worked fine. I mean the thoughts spinning around in my head," Tia says as she stares at the floor. "The doctors weren't sure I'd have full use of my hand again, or even my arm actually. Potential nerve damage. When they told me that, I completely lost it." She turns to the front wall, to the shelf of oversized vases. "I broke my best work from *Outliers*. Smashed them to bits."

"You smashed your stuff? Your great big vases?" I can't believe it. I just assumed she never finished making the rest, not that she trashed them.

"Yeah. The exhibit had seven total. And that's what's left," she says, tipping her can at the three huge vases she had shown me before. "I couldn't stand to see the exhibit so *whole* while I was so messed up, so I turned some of it back into dust. The gallery director asked me why, but I didn't know. She was absolutely furious, but at the time," Tia turns back to me, "it's what I needed."

I sit in stunned silence. I never exactly thought about why I couldn't stop cutting, just that I didn't want to. Even with all the angst and secrets, doing it and then watching the scabs crust up, even with all the drama it created—screwing up things with Amber and Elle, messing with my head, and weirdest of all, needing to cut deeper and longer to get the rush—I kind of liked it. I always liked it, from that very first night in the closet.

And I liked it for a simple reason: it *worked*.

"But deep down you hated breaking your vases, right?"

Tia nods slowly, staring at nothing the way she does when she's in thought.

"I don't. That's the difference."

"I don't believe you," she says, leaning towards me, her eyes bright and flushed.

"Seriously. I feel better when I, um, cut." I whisper the last part. For some reason, naming what I do, actually saying it out loud, makes me cringe like I'm blowing my cover, even though it's way too late for that.

"Fine. So it makes you feel better. You can find some *other thing* that makes you feel better. And you will. This is your doctor's job, to help you figure out what that other thing might be." Tia gets up and goes to the half-door where Chloe has begun scratching to be let in again. She rushes in, tail wagging, tongue everywhere, slobbering all over my shoes.

Coming back and leaning across the table, Tia holds out the same rough and ragged hands I have watched twirl oven-hot liquid into art. I look her in the eye, reach across, and hold on.

NINETEEN

I squeeze past a horde of freshmen gathered around an ancient, cracked-open PC whose guts spill all over the counter, two juniors stuffed in the sound booth recording voiceovers, and Adam-the-AV cranking an enormous roll of green paper—Marshall High's version of a green screen—back into a tube on the wall before I see Amber and Elle, heads bent close together over a monitor in the far corner.

I'm not surprised to see Mr. Rockstad's better lab jammed with students. Anybody with an interest in computers, gaming, media, or anything related to studio production rushes the room during Free Study or lunch. Actual computer classes happen in a high-tech media room off to the side while the rest of Marshall's nerd population geek out on the slick equipment in the main space.

"No way!" Amber shakes her head, laughing. "I am not calling us 'penetration testers.' That's just too pervy." When a D&D dork at the next computer station looks over and smiles, she rolls her eyes.

"I like 'ethical hackers.' It's got that straight-up, old-school IBM feel, although it does sound like we're a couple of middle-aged white guys in ties." Elle sits back in her chair, tapping a pen on her chin. I see their project abstract, the shortened version of the paper they have to hand in with their program, on the screen between them. My logo *should have* been at the top of the page, with screen caps of the website and its URL making up the bottom. I swallow hard.

"Tiger Team."

Elle and Amber spin in their seats.

"Hey, Kat." Elle tries a weak smile while Amber ducks her head and suddenly finds a mountain of invisible cat hair to pick off her sweater.

Tiger Team. Slang for ethical hackers, 'white hats,' the good guys. We learned it a few years back after reading an exposé about a tiger team busting a dog fighting ring by discovering exploited weaknesses in the computer system of a national animal rights organization. Cool stuff.

"So, you guys working on your abstract?" Well *that* was brilliant. Obviously. That's why it's on the screen.

"Yeah." Amber finally looks at me. She takes a breath. "What are you doing here? Is everything ok?" Her forehead crinkle creases in concern. Only Amber.

"I'm fine, just wanted to stop by and, you know, maybe talk? But only if you guys have time. I know you have tons to do, so it's cool if you're busy." I back up, trip over Amber's messenger, step on some kid's foot and knock over his binder, all in one step.

"Hey, yo!" The kid yanks his foot back while snatching up papers that flutter around.

"Sorry!"

"Oh my god, stop moving!" Elle jumps up and, half-hugging me, she drags over an extra chair and plunks me down. "Just stay there before you trash the place."

I sit down and make myself look at them, at my besties I haven't really talked to in however long. Amber and Elle look fine. Actually, they look great. They always did rock their stuff under pressure and now they're practically glowing. I'm glad. They've worked hard for this, so if I'm bummed I'm not a part, well, too bad so sad. Time to suck it up. I grab for the orange triangle in my pocket and then let it go and put my hands in my lap instead.

"Kat..." Elle starts, tapping her pen on the keyboard before Amber reaches over and takes it.

"You read the flyer." Amber looks straight at me when she says it. No crinkle, no hesitation, just pure Amber.

"It's awesome. I knew you guys would get it all finished in time." I try to hold my hands steady in my lap.

"We weren't sure until just last week," Elle says.

"Yeah, some guys from LaCordia High have something called 'White Hats Off' that has some ethical hack components, but it doesn't matter. I'm happy with our submission." Amber fiddles with Elle's pen. "We missed you."

"No one to do latte runs, right?" I force a laugh and try to smile. Somewhere after my third can of fizzy water and right before my arms were about to fall off from holding up the huge Swedish overlay vase, Tia convinced me I should talk to Amber and Elle. Clear the air. Get my friends back. Stop being a jerk. But I don't know how.

"We could maybe live without the caffeine," Amber says, so quietly I have to lean in to hear her. "But a logo and the website would have been helpful seeing as you did kind of *promise* them."

Ouch. I close my eyes. Listening to all the odd sounds that fill the computer lab—clicking keys, mumbled whispers, laughs, the silent-electric hum of white noise—I wonder, again how I have gotten here, so far away from where I began. A keyboard clicks right next to my ear.

"Tiger Team." Elle hits the enter key with a big

flourish.

"You think they'll go for that?" Amber looks skeptical.

"Of course. It's a legit term. We're good." Elle and Amber look at each other and something I don't understand passes between them. But I'm out of time, so now or never.

"You guys..." I barely begin the world's biggest apology when the bell rings for 6th period. Elle and Amber begin packing up books and legal pads that spread across almost three cubicles. I stand there like a doof, waiting.

"Kat, you better hurry up if you're going to get to Clarick's before late bell. She's such a tyrant," Amber says, dropping uncapped pens into her messenger.

"And a troll..." adds Elle.

I can't go to class if I don't say *something*.

"You guys, look, I'm...sorry." I must sound desperate because they both stop packing and look up.

"We can't talk about this right now. We're all going to be monstrously late," Amber says, turning away. Yeah, I'm not imagining it. She's definitely pissed. Sixth period students start to pour through the lab doors.

"Meet us by Betsy after 7th, ok?" When Elle says this Amber shoots her a look she thinks I don't see, something we never would have done to each other before. "Kat? Hello?" Elle waves her hands in front of my face. "After 7th period. Betsy. Nod yes."

"Um, yeah. Sure. Ok." They head for the hall and take off in opposite directions while I wind my way to chemistry, Clarick, and the Joey/Taylor jerk combo, two rowers I'd rather never see again.

I lean on Betsy as waves of upperclassmen pour out of Marshall's front doors headed for scrimmages, home, band practice, fast food, part-time jobs and, I soon learn, dress shopping. By the time Elle drops the bomb we're speeding down Route 1, going way too fast for me to open Betsy's backdoor and leap. Too bad.

"And then we were like, 'Yeah, why not? We kicked butt. We should celebrate.' So we got tickets and decided we needed awesome outfits." Elle peeks back at me in the rearview, huge smile on her face. I feel lost. Dress shopping for the Harvest Dance isn't the most horrible idea, but still. We've gone to other school dances and had a decent time, but that was before. And we always planned it *together*. I feel lost, and kind of stuck.

Amber strains towards me from the passenger seat, strangled by Betsy's seatbelts.

"So, are you coming?"

"Am I...?"

"The dance. Are. You. Coming." Her look challenges me to say anything other than yes. Not a look I'm used to coming from my best friend. "It's this Friday, there are still tickets left, and I can drive." I swallow the lump in my throat. I deserve this. Tension has gotten thick. And I haven't even really apologized yet.

"I don't know."

Amber turns away. I stare at the marks where Betsy's seatbelt has dug into her neck and will her to turn back and *say something*.

"Come on!" I say, not a little desperately, "I had no idea it was this Friday and we haven't exactly been talking."

"It wouldn't matter even if we had planned it,"

Amber mumbles. I catch it, though.

Elle makes a slow turn into the mall parking lot, driving to the higher-end department stores. By the time we weave through the lot, find a parking space, and come to a stop, I'm crying. Amber's tough expression splits right open when she gets out and sees me hunched in the back seat.

Oblivious, Elle heads straight for the store while Amber opens Betsy's back door and crawls in beside me.

"At some point she's going to realize she's talking to herself. Give it a minute," Amber says. Reaching the store doors, Elle looks around frantically, then hurries back to Betsy.

"Hey, what the hell?" When Elle sees us in the backseat, she crawls in on my other side. The three of us hug and then end up crying until we can't breathe, not saying much at first.

"Ok, look, I need to start with I'm sorry." I manage to squeak out a few things—I know they're both mad, I'm proud they got their project done for NECOM, I'm sorry I flaked on my part and then ditched the Con too. Then I mention how I thought my dad brought his girlthing to Piccollo's.

"Oh my god. That's just wrecked." Amber's eyes get horror-movie big.

"What did your shrink say? About your dad and all of it?" Elle asks.

"I don't know, just that he's trying but he messed up or something." I shrug. "It's all just too much...without you guys." I start to tear up again.

"Kat," Amber swallows, "look, you know we love you. You're just acting so weird this year." When I open my mouth to protest she holds up her hand. "I *know* you're going through a lot. I totally get that. Just...you're making it hard to be around. You blow off everything we plan and you won't even hang out. You don't even answer your phone anymore. It's like you don't want to be near us."

I don't know what to say, because it's all true.

Amber holds my hand. "Why are you avoiding us? It's like you turned into somebody else this summer."

I look at Elle on my left and Amber on my right. The three of us hold hands, connected by memories, school, love, and a zillion other things.

"I did." I shove used tissues into my bag.

"What do you mean?" Elle says, trying to catch my eye but I shake my head. "What happened?" Now she sounds frantic. Sandwiched between my besties, I decide to jump.

"So you guys remember when I went to Green Day?"

"Yeah," Elle says, "with Joey. That weekend I was at my gramps' and Amber was somewhere, computer camp maybe." Amber nods.

"Well..." I hesitate.

"I thought you guys had fun," Amber says.

"Um, we did," I say, slowly. "But we were kind of trashed and...had an accident on the way home."

"I didn't know that!" Elle squeaks.

"No one did. I didn't say anything, not even to my mom and dad. It was kind of bad..."

"So you've been avoiding us because Joey had an accident after the concert? Why didn't you just tell us? Are you ok? You both seem fine..." Elle looks puzzled.

"I'm fine," I lie. "And I should have told you guys but

I was too embarrassed. I mean, how dumb, right? So, yeah." It even sounds lame to me.

"You and Joey have a fender bender after a show this summer and that makes you decide to switch your classes and stop hanging out?" Amber asks. "Somebody please help me understand exactly *how* that makes sense."

"Amber, it wasn't a 'fender bender.' It was horrible," I choke, starting to cry even harder. Amber's eyes, usually the softest brown, look hard in the falling light.

We jump when Elle's phone starts pinging. "Hey," she says, checking the text, "I'm sorry but my mom wants to know if we're going to be long. She needs me to run an errand."

"It's ok," I say, wiping my eyes, "I can't be late so we should do this shopping thing if we're going to."

"Fine," Amber says, climbing out of Betsy. She won't meet my eyes. We head towards the mall, red-eyed, wrinkled, sniffly. Not speaking.

I'm not even sure we're all still friends.

TWENTY

"Can I see?" Mom sounds frantic behind my door.

"Just...can you wait a second? *Please?*" Unreal. You might think I'm headed to my own wedding.

"I'm just excited, Kat." I hear mumbling in the hall. "Honey? Pete's leaving to pick up Meghan and I want some pictures before he goes. I'll see you downstairs." Ah yes, the all-American couple, off to get trashed at some pre-party.

I blot my lips one more time and look in the mirror. Not bad. The long black dress definitely makes me look taller. Well, that and the strappy 4" platform heels. I feel ok. *This will be ok.* Breathe. The final touch: a black velvet choker that sets off the super-long silver gloves.

The front door slams as I grab my shawl and wristlet and creep down the hall. I can't avoid Mom, so I give up on stealth and clomp down the steps, holding on to the bannister. I know Mom hates the shoes. One bonus about being in therapy: you mention wanting to do something normal, like go to a school dance, and parents act like you've won an Olympic gold. If I really played it right, I probably could have gotten a car out of it. For tonight, I'm good with my killer dress and platforms. The elbow-length silver gloves were, believe it or not, Mom's idea. They cover everything from fingertips up.

I couldn't exactly try on cocktails dresses with my messed-up arms. When I told Mom that Elle and Amber wanted me to go to the Harvest Dance and that I had seen a really awesome black dress, she didn't blink twice. Just handed me her VISA and ordered me back to the mall. But when I explained there was *no way* I could wear a dress with tiny straps, she shoved some meatballs into the microwave for Pete and dragged me back to the mall herself, grabbing the glittery shawl and gloves on the way to the dressing room.

I hadn't seen Mom in that good of a mood in forever. We found an awesome wristlet and, against her better judgment but smiling the whole time, Mom also let me get the ridiculously expensive platforms.

"Oh, Kat," Mom turns around and starts to sniffle, "I wish Dad could see you!"

"Yeah, well..." I shrug. I don't want to spoil the mood, so I don't say anything. Tonight I refuse to deal with my dad, his girlthing, any of it. Dresses and dancing, that's my focus.

I hear a knock at the back door, followed by a bark. I bolt for the kitchen and nearly wipe out. Tia peeks in the window while Chloe fidgets on her leash.

"Hey!" I open the door and step back before Chloe can plant wet paws on me.

"Kat, you look *gorgeous*!" Tia beams at me and I feel happy, like I've finally done something right. "Seriously, you are beautiful, sweetie." She starts tearing up and wipes her eyes with a hand that happens to be holding a doggy poop bag. We burst out laughing.

"Thanks. What do you think?" I lift one foot to show off my heels.

"*Killer*." Tia smiles wider than I have ever seen.

"Do you want to come in? Amber and Elle aren't here yet."

"Thanks, but someone has to pee," she says, shaking Chloe's leash. "We just wanted to see you before you left. Hello, Margaret!" Tia yells around me, towards the living room.

"You know my mom?"

Tia cocks her head and half-shrugs. "We *are* neighbors, Kat. It's not unheard of."

"I know. I just..."

"Hello, Tia!" yells Mom from the other room. "Can I offer you some coffee? I have a pot of that dark roast from Piccollo's you recommended."

"Thank you, but no. Chloe and I are headed for our walk. Have a good night!" Now it's my turn to look struck.

"You've had entire conversations with my mom?"

Tia just smiles and nudges Chloe down the porch steps. "Have an awesome night, Kat. Come over tomorrow if you feel like it. And take notes. I want to hear about everyone's dresses."

"You want to hear about *dresses*?"

"Sure. I like couture as much as anyone. I do clean up pretty well, you know." Tia winks and laughs as she steps into the shadows with Chloe by her side. As soon as I close the back door I hear voices in the living room.

Amber looks amazing in the copper mermaid dress she found hidden behind some frumpy sale stuff and Elle looks like a movie star in a short red cupcake skirt. The three of us look really good.

"Oh, girls!" Mom squeals between camera snaps. "You all look so beautiful!"

"Thanks, Mrs. Morgan." Amber and Elle smile awkwardly, and I remember that the last time they saw Mom, she was grilling them about helping me cut.

"Ok, Mom, see you later." I herd the girls to the door.

"Have fun, girls! Kat, home by midnight, please."

"'K, Mom. Bye." We pile into Amber's mom's car.

"Your mom seems ok." Amber pulls out onto York Avenue and we head for school. She hasn't mentioned the conversation in Betsy all week, and I really just hope she'll drop it completely.

Elle pokes her head up between the two front seats. "Kat, I'm glad you came." She smiles and reaches for my hand. "And I vote no family crap tonight. Just fun!" She bounces up and down in her seat.

"Agreed."

The gym looks insanely good. Marshall's Spirit Sluts take their gym decorating duties very seriously. Shelley said she overheard Cassidy Falls telling the committee that anyone who even suggested streamers would sit out the first three games of the season. I guess she wasn't kidding. In the center of the room, live trees surround a pond with a tiny waterfall. Hundreds of bright orchids fill every open space and shimmer to the thumping bass beat. We spot Cassidy and Traves holding court by the stage.

"How do you think they got him to come? I'd feel kind of weird, after the funeral and everything," Elle whispers as we try not to stare at his wheelchair.

"Take a peek at Cassidy's dress. No contest there." Amber snorts as Cassidy comes into view wearing the lowest cut dress I have ever seen on someone not a Victoria's Secret model. We watch as the lacrosse team hovers around Traves' chair, slapping his back and making small talk while sneaking looks at Cassidy's tits.

"Do you think they're going to play this all night?" Elle frowns at the dance beat. "I'm kind of hoping for some old-school stuff."

"I wouldn't hold your breath on that one, Elley," says Amber, staring across the room. "Hey, cool!" A half dozen photo booths line up across the south hallway.

"Holy crap. Check out Mr. Miles!" Elle shrieks and covers her mouth. In the opposite corner Mr. Miles is doing some kind of horrific herky-jerky thing. "Is he having a seizure?" she yells above the music. But no, my geometry teacher is trying to dance.

A tall blond I recognize from Computer Science Club appears in front of us, standing awkwardly on one foot, scratching his chin. "Hey, Amber, you, uh..." he half-asks, pointing at the dance floor.

"Yeah, sure." Amber shrugs and moves towards the crowd of jouncing bodies.

"Hey, Kat, I see Mr. Rockstad. I should tell him..."

"Just go, Elle," I laugh. "I'll be by the photo booths when you get tired of nerd speak." Elle says a nasty word in French and blows me a kiss as she marches off in her cupcake skirt. I clomp across the dance floor to lean against a photo booth, noticing lights strung through rafters, how the soft green trees drip actual leaves, the way the waterfall catches the light, and my friends looking glittery and smiley. Crazy night. But crazy-good for once.

I look around and spot the rest of the usual suspects, the crew jocks, and members of the Quidditch Club walking around, unbelievably, with brooms. I catch Elle's eye across the room—are you *seeing* this?—and start laughing, when I hear it. At first I'm sure the pounding music is messing with me. But then I hear it again. Behind me. A guy and a girl in a photo booth. They're laughing and sound pretty trashed.

"C'mon. You are so uptight. You need to relax," he says again. The girl mumbles something, maybe *no* or *ok* or *I don't know*. Well, that sounds familiar. "One hit and you will feel like a fucking rock star! You *know* you want to. God, you look so beautiful tonight," he says while she giggles. Then a pause. "There ya' go!"

I know this! I know that voice. I know those words. I know how this works. Like using the Pythagorean theorem, or conjugating French verbs, or denaturing a protein. Step one, step two, step three...

He'll take her out to his car where they'll drink and make out while he slowly undresses her. She's so trashed she won't even mind being undressed, flying on X, going down on a guy she likes but doesn't really know, in a rusted green Toyota in a parking lot. Then he'll tell her how much he likes her. When they're done, they'll drive off, completely wasted, and ruin lives.

I did. I did all that with Joey. So will this girl.

I slip sideways between two booths as Joey shoves the curtain aside, stumbling out and into the hallway with Paula, guys from the crew team looking over and laughing. For a split second, I think they're laughing at me.

But, no, Joey half-dances, half-drags Paula across the floor towards the door. It takes forever. They stop every few feet to kiss roughly, Paula ramming her tongue into his mouth, grabbing his junk. Joey throws his hands up, acting stupid and helpless, laughing.

Taylor, dateless and drunk, grinds on Paula as she passes by hanging off Joey's arm. Joey carefully guides her around two chaperones and through the doors that lead to the parking lot. I don't see Amber or Elle. Just colors, dresses, trees, the tinkly waterfall. I hear noise, but can't tell what I'm hearing. The music pushes in at me, making me hold my head.

I need to get out of here. I'm drowning. I want to open myself up and crawl inside. I have to do something. I ache for my orange triangle, for a paper clip, for anything. I hold my arms against myself so I don't fly apart. I want to slice, to open myself up, cut and cut until there are only ribbons left. Until my legs bleed a river, until I see bone and veins and muscle...

"Kat? You ok?" Shelley leans over me. I'm still pinched between the photo booths. I scrabble to get up and knock a line of pictures from the slot. Four perfect little rectangles on a long strip.

"Joey..." I say breathlessly.

"Yeah, I saw them," she laughs, waving at the dance floor where the rest of the school thrashes to an old grunge song. *Elle will like that*, I think, feeling crazy that I'm even thinking about the music right now. "They looked ready to do it right here."

I shove the picture strip into my glove and drag myself up. "He pinged her." I'm out of breath, like I've just run a race.

"What?"

"Joey. He had X, and he talked Paula into dropping it with him."

Shelley shrugs. "Joey likes to party and Paula likes Joey so not exactly news. Like you wouldn't know? You *did* date the guy."

I stare at her, openmouthed. "What? We only went to a concert one time."

"I guess...Joey told Taylor about you, and I made the mistake of going to the movies with him once. He gossips worse than the Spirit Sluts." My head spins. "So what's the problem? You guys still dating or something?"

I stumble, turning away from Shelley, the lights, the music. I walk blindly down the hallway, past lockers and classrooms, away from all sound until I reach the metal security grate near the nurse's office. I dig out my phone. Dial. She said I could call, *should* call, any time. It rings four times, five times. Soon I'll get voicemail. What the hell am I going to say?

"Hello, this is Dr. Caleno." I wait for the rest of the voicemail, for the beep. *"Hello?"* My god, she picked up. The woman actually picked up. I take a shaky breath and swallow.

"Dr. Caleno...it's Kat. Kat Morgan?" I wait a heartbeat to make sure she heard me.

"Kat, how can I help you?" she sounds insanely calm.

"I'm sorry, I know it's late, it's just that I have a problem."

"It's fine, Kat. Tell me what's wrong."

"I...so Joey, the guy I went to that concert with last summer when my dad was so mad? Well, he just...dropped X with Paula."

"Who's Paula? And where are you?"

Damn, she probably thinks I'm trashed too. "Paula is his date. I'm at school, at a dance." "Ok..." she says slowly.

"They went outside so I don't know where they are now. I don't know what to do. Just, the last time he drove after drinking and doing X..." I can barely catch my breath.

"I need you to breathe, Kat. I'm going to hang up now so I can take care of this."

"Wait, what should I do now?" I stumble over my words.

"Well, seeing as you're all dressed up at a dance, go find your friends and...dance."

"You're not fucking serious..." I start to say as the line goes dead.

TWENTY-ONE

Dawn spreads like a bruise over my comforter, making me want to throw up at the idea of facing today. I lift my head from my desk where I've fallen asleep, dress pooling around my ankles, mascara caked and sticky on my face from crying. I notice my shoes across the room but don't remember taking them off. I barely remember coming home.

What a mess. I've ruined the whole night for all of us. Making them leave the dance, crying all the way home. Not exactly the kind of sleepovers we used to have.

Amber sits up on the bed, yawning, wearing pjs she dug out of my drawer. Her dress sits in a twisted tangle on the floor next to Elle who slumps on an oversized pillow in her skirt and a Marshall High sweatshirt, eyes closed. It feels like we're all holding our breath but I know that can't be right because Elle just let out a sigh.

"Kat?" Amber rubs her eyes.

"Yeah?"

"Are you ok?"

Elle opens her eyes. Apparently we're jumping right in.

"So...do you guys want some coffee?" I'm not exactly sure what to say next.

"Coffee?" Amber looks beaten down, her forehead crinkle standing out on her face. "No, I don't want coffee. Ok, I *do*, but totally not the point. Kat, what the hell was last night?" I look down, out the window, anywhere but at my friends. "You know we love you, right?" She crosses her arms in a way that I recognize from when she's figuring out code, challenging it to give up secrets.

I finally hear Mom somewhere downstairs, jingling keys, getting ready to go to the bakery. It must be uber-early, too early for this conversation.

"I'm sorry," I say. "I know I totally ruined the dance for you guys..."

"Forget. The. Dance." Elle unfolds herself from the floor. Ignoring the skirt plastered to her in a crumpled mess, she marches over to me, tripping over yoga pants, dirty socks, and my French book. She looks furious. "Look, we know you're bummed about Joey and Paula and, not to sound bitchy, but *why do you even care*? Do you still like him or something?" Her voice softens on the last part but the idea of liking Joey feels so far from the truth, I actually snort.

"No, I don't like him."

"Then what's going on?" Amber asks. "I've never seen you so messed up. It's like you weren't even here. We find you crying by the nurse's office, so we come home and you won't talk, just start rocking like someone who's lost it. Last night was scary." I'm reminded of the beginning of the school year, of Amber standing outside my locker, asking me if I was going to flake on her again. If she only knew.

"They were going to leave, drive away..." I whisper. Amber and Elle exchange glances.

"Who?" Amber asks.

I start to shake, small tremors running through me, making me jerk around. "Last summer, after the concert..." I begin, as Elle backs up and joins Amber on the bed, "we were driving home..." I stop. No way I can do this. People always *think* they want to hear the truth, the horrible stuff, but then once they know, they bolt and don't look back.

"The night of the concert was just really bad," I say quietly.

"You never even talked about it. And," Elle spins her arms in frustration, "what does that have to do with last night and all this weird shit that's going on?"

I start to try to explain when Amber explodes.

"I'm tired of this, Kat! I'm trying to be supportive, really, but if you want to keep your secrets, well, then..." Amber gets off the bed and starts to grab her stuff strewn across the room.

"Amber, wait," Elle says, panicky.

"No, I'm done. I'm not doing this anymore," she snaps, stuffing her necklace and some bangles into a backpack as she heads for the bedroom door.

"We killed someone!" I choke. Time stops as Amber drops her pack and Elle pulls the comforter around her.

"After the show. Joey was trashed and there was a guy and...and...I think we killed him. We ran him over."

"*What?*" Amber shouts. I nod silently, numb. I should feel relieved. I don't.

"You ran over some guy in the parking lot? Who was he?" Elle whispers in a rush.

"No, not there. It happened later. Near Palmer Park."

"Holy crap," Amber says, mouth open. "Just...ok, what *exactly* happened? You and Joey were drinking..."

"Yeah, we, um...had a few beers, dropped some X, hooked up, and then left the show..." I look up to see Elle and Amber sitting with wide eyes.

Elle looks like I've slapped her. "You dropped X with Joey. Which, by the way, you said you would never do. Hooked up with him. Ran over some guy. And then *lied about it* for the rest of the summer. Are you kidding me?"

"I'm sorry! I didn't know what to do." My voice catches in my throat.

Elle shakes her head. "This is unreal."

"Wait," Amber rubs her face, "when did the hitting part happen?"

"Down by Palmer Park there was this old guy walking his dog. We tried to swerve but, something happened, and...we hit him. And then," I stop to take a shaky breath, "we drove away. I told Joey to stop, but he said the guy was fine, that we'd call 911 later. When we got to my house," I choke, "there was blood and stuff on the car."

Snot and tears mix with old mascara and roll down my face while my best friends in the world sit like zombies, blinking at the rising sun pouring into the window.

Nobody says a word.

TWENTY-TWO

I stumble into homeroom right at the bell juggling a yogurt, one lone mitten, a crinkled chem lab, and my messenger bag.

"Ms. Morgan." McCallister nods at me. "Glad you could join us for morning announcements." I resist rolling my eyes as I drop my junk and dig for my phone. Dr. Caleno has left a voicemail. Weird. She's never called me before. Seeing her number makes my stomach flutter, but not exactly in an awesome way. If I listen to it now I risk having McCallister confiscate the phone. Amber leans over.

"What's up? Why are you so late? Are you ok?"

"Almost rode in with Pete," I whisper, as announcements start, "except the idiot..." but then I stop. Most mornings, announcements begin with a Student Council rep pushing some bake sale or fundraiser for the Kerry Sumner Memorial Fund. Today Mrs. Caine, front office secretary, is droning *Katherine Morgan will report to the front office. Katherine Morgan, to the front office, please.*

"Oh my god, what now?" Amber whispers as the whole class turns to eye me. I stuff my phone in my pocket, take the hall pass McCallister holds out to me, and start walking.

Here we go.

I haven't been in Hunter's office since early in the semester. A huge banner for the Kerry Sumner Memorial Fund now hangs across the front counter where Madame Jolais drops junk from her mailbox into a recycling bin.

"*Bonjour, Katerine! Comment va-tu?*" she asks.

"Well..."

"Kat Morgan?" Mrs. Caine asks, looking up.

"Yes."

"He's waiting for you," she says, pointing at Hunter's closed door.

I look at Madame Jolais. "*Il va être une journée intéressante,*" I say. Madame winks.

"Mr. Hunter?" I knock and peek inside, heart practically beating out of my shirt. I can guess why I'm here, but that doesn't make it any easier. Hunter gestures to come in. He points at the chair in front of his desk and, as I sit, Bonsky comes tumbling in behind me, files slipping from her hands.

"Sorry I'm late, Mr. Hunter. We had what you would call an 'SAT crisis,'" she says using air quotes, "with one of the seniors, but we figured it out." She trails off at Hunter's look.

"Ah, ok. So..." Hunter looks like he'd rather be just about anywhere else. Join the club. "I know you've been seeing Dr. Lily Caleno and I asked you here today because of the phone call you made to her Friday evening during the Harvest Dance. She repeated some very serious accusations." Bonsky pops a Lifesaver and nods. "And I'd like to know what happened."

I think about Dr. Caleno's voicemail and wonder if she knew this would be happening this morning. Hunter leans back in his chair, making it groan slightly, as Bonsky sits forward.

"Ok," I start, "well... "

"You claimed something about drugs?" Hunter asks, frowning.

"I...yeah. I saw Joey Lawlor give Paula Conte X."

"X?"

"Ecstasy."

"You saw this? Where did they do this?" Hunter looks pissed.

"Well, I didn't *see it*-see it, I heard it. It happened in one of the photo booths. But that's not..."

"In a photo booth. You were in a photo booth with Mr. Lawlor and Ms. Conte when you saw this happen?" Hunter asks while Bonsky *tsk tsks* around her Lifesaver.

"No, I was next to the booth. Kind of between booths, and I recognized, um, the things he was saying to her." Hunter looks confused. "He talked her into dropping the X and then he dragged her to his car. I didn't think he should be driving..."

"He *dragged* her to his car? Did anyone else see this?"

"Yeah, everybody. Well, ok, not the dragging because he wasn't *literally* dragging her. They were kind of making out, headed for the doors..." A line of sweat pops out around my head like a halo and another snakes its way down my back, making my waffle tee stick to me. I feel hot, cold, and sick all at once as I realize that I sound like an idiot. I can tell Hunter thinks so too.

"I'm struggling with this, Kat," he says while he rubs his face. "I want to help, to stop any kind of illegal behavior, but this all seems very fuzzy. Dr. Caleno led me to believe you were witness to this incident, something serious enough to put a young man's sports career at risk."

I catch myself shredding my cuticles and force my hand into my lap. Hunter is worried about *Joey*? Two sharp knocks at Hunter's door make us all jump. Coach

Marlton, head of Marshall's varsity rowing crew, pushes it open. And glares.

"So you're Katherine Morgan," he says in a thick British accent as he runs his eyes over me. I know the horror stories from Pete, how Marlton would have them on the river in temperatures so cold their hands would freeze into position or make them do jump-squats until someone threw up. It always sounded so lame when Pete would complain—the poor varsity rower actually had to exercise—but now I can see why you'd sprint or do whatever this guy told you to.

"Coach, please come in," Hunter says. Marlton grabs a chair by the wall and drags it up to Hunter's desk. The way he looks at Hunter, I can tell he thinks he should be sitting behind the desk, not in front of it. Bonsky clears her throat nervously then starts chewing the dregs of her Lifesaver.

"I'll be brief, Mr. Hunter. I just need to know my stroke is cleared for Saturday's regatta." Hunter rubs his face with his bear paw again and pierces me with a look.

"Well, Coach, that's what we're trying to determine. Kat," Hunter says turning back to me, "what *exactly* did you see? Start at the beginning. You arrived at the dance..."

I tell Hunter how after Elle, Amber, and I got to the dance, I wandered over to the photo booths and heard Joey saying things to his date. How, when he and Paula stepped out of the booth, they sort of swayed their way over to the doors and left. And how Taylor followed them.

"Wait one moment," Marlton says, his accent taking on an edge, "you *think* you heard part of some conversation, then saw Mr. Lawlor accompanying his date outside and, from this, assume he is forcing drugs on this young lady?"

"No, that's not it...I was worried he was going to drive..."

"I'm sorry, Kat, but your cause and effect are a little shaky here." Hunter shakes his head.

"Ms. Morgan," Marlton says, standing, "when did *you* date Mr. Lawlor?"

Hunter raises his eyebrows. "You two dated?"

"We went on *one* date, last summer, and—"

"And, upset at the prospect of not being asked to the dance by a young man you still like, made serious accusations against him," Marlton says, satisfied.

"That's not it," I say as I accidentally knock my messenger bag off my lap. It lands upside down, spilling pens and class notes everywhere. The picture booth strip flutters and lands like a feather on top of the mess. "It's not about the X! That's not even the point..."

I can't read Marlton's face as he bends down and picks up the picture strip. He takes a long look.

"We're done here, Principal Hunter," Marlton says, standing, handing Hunter the picture strip. I already know what it shows: the first frame with Joey and Paula off-center, laughing, having fun...then an elbow, fuzzy skin, a flash of bright scarlet dress, waving hands. A lot of nothing. "Ms. Morgan," Marlton says quietly, "were I you I'd be very careful about my accusations lest you be prepared to discuss the intimacies of your own relationship with Mr. Lawlor."

I think I might be sick. "*What?*"

"Mr. Lawlor has shared with me details of your

relationship and, frankly, they give me pause. As for Ms. Conte, to my knowledge she has not registered any sort of complaint." He looks at Hunter who shakes his head. "As Antisthenes states, 'As iron is eaten by rust, so are the envious consumed by envy.' Think on that, Ms. Morgan." Marlton opens the door and swings it wide. "Mr. Hunter, Ms. Bonsky, good day."

And he's gone.

TWENTY-THREE

"What the *hell* are you doing?" Pete asks, slamming his backpack on the kitchen island hard enough to make my cereal bowl jump.

I brace myself and look up from my unfinished French homework. "Don't you have a date with Meghan in the parking lot?" I've got exactly 13 minutes before the bus comes to finish translating a short story about the trip Alice and Michele want to take to downtown Paris. No way will Madame Jolais excuse another late homework. And no way will Pete give me a ride to school. Especially not now. Not after yesterday.

"You're an asshole, Kat, and the whole school knows it." I start typing again but my stomach lurches. I knew this was coming. I've been ready ever since lunch yesterday when the comments from Paula Conte's table got so bad I left for the library. Chemistry wasn't much better. Taylor had told Shelley, making sure I could hear, that Joey was with Coach Marlton, having a conversation about the rest of his season "thanks to the big-mouthed bitch."

Pete shoves my book away from me. "Go to Hunter and take it back."

"It's none of your business." I keep my voice steady.

"Yeah, right. You're fucking with the crew team. Stop trying to get back at Joey just because he doesn't like you. That's totally pathetic." Pete grabs the milk from the fridge and drinks from the carton. "*You* are totally pathetic," he says with a milky burp.

"I'm not doing anything to the crew team. I told somebody what I saw. And *she* told Hunter, not me.

That's it." Like the crew team actually thinks I went to Hunter because Joey wouldn't date me? Yeah, right.

"Do you really think Joey is going to want to hook up after you narced on him?"

"I don't like Joey, Pete. I haven't liked him...for a long time."

"You're such a loser. You and your lesbo computer friends—"

"Shut up!"

Pete stomps out of the kitchen, leaving me with soggy cereal and seven minutes to finish my homework.

"You don't understand," I whisper to no one at all.

I see Elle and Amber waiting by Betsy and I can tell something is really wrong.

"Hey," I say, "What's going on?" They exchange looks.

"Um, Kat?" Amber says, looking ill, "You need to stay calm. Ok? Just remember you did the right thing." I stop walking.

"Ok, now you're freaking me out." That's when I notice. People around us are sneaking looks and snickering. I have a sudden, sick flashback to the start of the semester, to Pete, Joey, Taylor, and the other sportos huddled around Joey's Toyota, talking and laughing. Elle sighs.

"Something showed up last night in Marshall's InstaChat feed. You know how the admin leaves the feed open so people can post spirit pictures? Well..." Amber digs in her bag and pulls out her phone, pulling up the school's account. The first thing I notice about the upload is the thick black heading that says, 'RECANT' above a photo. It only takes me a second to recognize the white tee and Gap shorts, the perfectly manicured bright pink toes, the girl stretched out on the backseat, arms around some guy's waist, head thrown back, laughing hysterically. She's obviously having a kick-ass time, totally happy and wasted. Her tee is also mostly off and her shorts are unzipped.

Fuck.

Just as the homeroom warning bell rings, I see Pete and Meghan across the parking lot, leaning against the Jeep looking at Meghan's phone. Pete has no expression while Meghan just laughs and laughs. I look back down at Amber's phone in my hands. For a second I think *I wish I could still wear shorts. My legs looked pretty decent last summer.*

Then I start to cry.

My dad looks simultaneously helpless and livid as Bonsky leans over and hands me another tissue. Hunter shakes his head and grunts as he puts the flyer down on his desk. Worried that someone might miss the InstaChat mess, some asshole printed a few dozen copies of the upload and left them around the quad where the wind papered them against trees and trashcans.

"Mr. Morgan, we will do our very best to find out who created and distributed this photo. It is, of course, completely inappropriate..."

"It's the crew team," I interrupt. "They're mad. Not exactly a mystery." Hunter gives me a sharp look.

"According to my daughter, Principal Hunter," Dad says through clenched teeth, "Kat saw a drug interaction of some sort at a dance last week and this is retribution against her."

"We don't know that yet, Mr. Morgan. Kat provided us with details about what she believes happened at the Harvest Dance involving a boy in her class and another young lady."

"Who's the boy? Have you talked to him? Or the girl?"

"Yes, the young man is Joey Lawler and—"

"*Joey Lawlor?!*" My father roars so loudly, Ms. Bonsky actually gasps. "He's the little shit who brought Kat home drunk last summer."

"Mr. Morgan..." Hunter stutters. Dad turns and looks me straight in the eye.

"He did this, honey? He spread around this picture?" I chew the inside of my cheek when I see the look on his face. He doesn't look mad exactly, more like fierce.

"Well, the picture is from...um...that concert," I say, waiting for an explosion. But Dad just nods quietly. The change is scary.

"Kat is coming home with me." Dad stands and motions for me to do the same. "I want these flyers off this campus immediately. And the picture off that online account, whatever it is. And understand that we'll be having our own conversation with the Lawlor family. With our attorney present." Hunter raises his eyebrows. "My wife couldn't be here but I'll fill her in and we'll look forward to an update on how the school will be handling whoever did this." Hunter looks very tired.

We drive in silence for almost 10 minutes when Dad finally starts. "Kat," he starts. *Please. Don't. Not now.* "Why didn't you tell Mom or me about drugs at the dance?"

"I don't know. I figured school would handle it." I feel Dad look at me.

"Principal Hunter said you called your counselor, Dr. Caleno..."

"That's what she's for, Dad."

"Right." Dad sighs.

"I don't really want to talk to Joey, Dad. Do we even *have* a lawyer?"

"Not really."

"But you told Hunter..."

"I know. I'm mad. Hunter is letting that kid walk around school after he...that's just wrong."

Dad stays silent until we turn into our neighborhood. I grab for the door as we pull up our drive. "Please. Wait." He takes a big breath. "I've made mistakes. And I realize you're upset with Mom and me, about things you overheard last summer." I meet Dad's eyes. "Yes, Mom and I know you and Pete have heard us fighting these past few months. It would have been hard to miss. And I'm sorry for that. But, Kat, I want you to be ok. That's why I got so mad when you came home drunk from that damn concert. My girl, with some asshole who only wanted..." My dad hiccups and starts to cry.

My dad. *Crying.*

I reach into my pocket, but only find lint. Orange triangle? Panty drawer. Stuffed in there after Dr. Caleno suggested I stop carrying around things I use to cut myself. I need to get inside the house. Out of this car. Anywhere but here.

I unfold a copy of the flyer I've been clenching in my hand. My legs are thin. Pretty. Tan. From a time when I didn't know how pushpins and paperclips and cuticle scissors could make such thick lumps of healed-over skin. My legs looked good.

"Kat," Dad sniffs, gently turning my face, "I'm here to help you however I can."

"Sure, Dad."

"Listen to me," he says, "whatever that boy did to you that night...we can get through this." He looks at the flyer in my hands and I see pain glaze his expression.

Oh, Daddy, it wasn't like that.

My heart bangs loudly as he puts his cool, dry lips on my forehead and holds me. The flyer slips from my clammy hands to the car floor.

TWENTY-FOUR

Dust motes dance across the room and I focus on the *pling pling* of the harpsichord pouring out of the speakers. When Dr. Caleno held up the Beethoven CD I had shrugged. Sure, whatever. A familiar calico with a butterscotch face eyes me from her window seat perch. What the hell is that cat doing here? Weird.

Slow and steady breaths. I know what I need to do.

I shrug off my coat. Dr. Caleno says the usual stuff, *How are you?* and *How was your week?* But I say nothing, just sit down and make an executive decision. Showtime.

I shove up my sleeves, sucking in my breath as cool air hits my raw, puckered skin and goose bumps rise. I avoid Dr. Caleno's face as I pull my bootcuts up to my thighs and lean back against the couch. I feel green velvet against the backs of my legs, a new sensation. Usually, the only thing I feel against my tortured skin is clothing, never air or light.

I sit, frozen. Exposed. Waiting for her judgment. Dr. Caleno glances at me and breaks into a small smile. "Let's talk about this."

"Pretty gross, right?" I say as I stare beyond her, out the round window behind her desk to a woolly bush that bursts with big purple and green leaves.

"You certainly have some scars," she says softly, not unkindly, "but I'd like to talk about this flyer first."

"The flyer?" Her words snap me back. I was expecting something about my body, about the scars, how they're so gross. She would never use such an un-PC word, but I can't believe she doesn't want to say *anything* about them. "The flyer," I say again. Dr. Caleno nods, laying a copy of the RECANT paper across her desk.

"Where did you get that?" I ask, shocked.

She lifts her shoulders into a slow and elaborate shrug. "Does it matter?"

It's my turn to shrug and look away. I can almost feel the room breathing as she waits for me to speak. "I think Joey made it. He'll probably get suspended from crew. It showed up on my school's InstaChat. And somebody printed out a bunch."

Caleno taps her pen to her eyebrow. "That's unfortunate."

I sigh. "Yup."

"Where was this taken?"

I hesitate. "At the Green Day concert. Probably while we were hanging out in his car."

"Do you remember him taking it?" I say nothing. She looks at it again before laying it back on her desk. "This is the night your dad mentioned to me, when he was concerned because you came home so drunk."

"Yeah, it was kind of a bad night. We were drinking and stuff and it just...wasn't good."

"What's that mean?"

"After the show, we were having a beer waiting for the lot to clear, when Joey said we should do some X, that it would be fun. That's probably when he took it." I wasn't going to talk about any of this—not a word—but I just don't care anymore. Dr. Caleno roots around in a drawer as she talks. "Ok, you went to a show, drank, dropped X, and...?" This is not why I'm here. "Kat?"

"I don't know. We hung out for a while..." I hold my arms against myself, stunned and heartbroken. If telling

Amber and Elle felt hellish, this feels deadly.

But I am so tired. I just can't anymore.

My secret, shoved down into a small ball of guilt, floods my mouth for the second time that week, pours out. I look directly at Dr. Caleno. "And then I think we killed someone."

I look down and realize I still have my sleeves pushed to my shoulders and my pant legs up around my knees, like some sick sideshow. I yank down my sleeves, scratching myself, not caring.

Dr. Caleno smirks from her desk. "Try again, kiddo."

Huh? What the hell does that mean?

She flips open a heavy blue folder and starts reading. "'On 17 July at approximately 23:48 a Caucasian male, identified as Gus Hardwick, was found disoriented by a jogger near Palmer Park. Injuries sustained include lacerations to face and hands, and broken right femur. Victim claimed a car (make and model unidentified), sped up and hit his dog. Skid marks suggest loss of control of vehicle. Dog was found unharmed at the scene.' There's more, but that's the general gist."

The man we killed...was alive?

"But when we got to my house," I say, unbelieving, sitting up, "there was blood on the car. A lot of blood."

"Yes, I imagine there was. Head wounds, even slight ones, bleed profusely." Dr. Caleno sits quietly, totally calm, like batshit-crazy happens to her every day. And then I realize...

"Where did you get that?" I ask, pointing at the police report. "Why do you have it? How do you...did Amber call you or something?" but I know she didn't.

No one called her.

In that second, I see Dr. Caleno bending time, I taste the same ashy fire and blazing light that sometimes scares the shit out of me in my dreams. The flames flare hot orange and red, racing towards me, dancing, singing, screaming.

I flash back to Ms.Wu's lecture on gamma waves, brain patterns that vibrate so high only monks meditating for 20 years reach the untapped space where the dimensions actually exist. The thought doesn't even make sense. My shrink isn't some monk with superpowers, just a weirdo with too many cats...but still.

"If you and Joey had called 911 that night, you would have known this man was alive. Joey would have been charged with a DUI. Wouldn't that have been better?"

Dr. Caleno leans towards me over her desk and, even from the couch I feel the fierce, terrifying energy that pulses around and through her. Her usually soft hazel eyes disappear into a pool of black. *Damn.*

"Would getting into trouble that night have been better or worse than trying to carve the guilt out of your skin and bone for the last 5 months?"

I sit speechless.

"I asked you a question. *Would it have been better or worse, Katherine?*"

My god, what a bitch. "Why are you being so mean to me?"

"What else do you remember from that night?"

"What? I told you. We were messed up and Joey was probably going too fast and...we hit the guy and his dog. Or I guess we didn't hit the dog. I don't know. Whatever." I can't catch my breath.

"Do you know why most people self-injure?" she

asks, leaning back in her chair while pushing around some papers, suddenly calm. I don't move.

"They need a release, a distraction from their emotions. So," she says, walking to her plant to touch leaves and check water, "are you ready to tell me about those scars?"

I have no clue where this is going. "I've screwed up my skin, mostly on my arms and legs, and some on my stomach. I'd think about the man and his dog and just..."

"What do you use to cut yourself?" I stop for a second before answering. The whole thing feels surreal, like we're discussing irregular French verbs or a new cupcake flavor at Mom's bakery.

"Um, pushpins. Sometimes cuticle scissors. Paperclips if I'm at school." She turns and looks right through me. "And there's this triangle..."

At home, I skate through the kitchen and head to my room, ducking Mom's questions about my session and Pete's dagger eyes as he shoves Oreos into his mouth. I try not to notice Mom's tired, puffy face. Dad showed her the flyer. I heard her crying in the downstairs bathroom after everyone had gone to bed.

I yank open my panty drawer and dig out the triangle. I study the art glass for the billionth time, turning it over in my hands. Even with eyes closed, it feels like daylight, the color of ripe fruit and warm sun. Too pretty to be used for something so ugly. And it's not even mine.

I tuck it away and look around my room. Clothes and books lay everywhere. Dirty socks and t-shirts cover the floor. My Harvest Dance dress sits crumpled in the corner. I should clean up. I should do a lot of things.

Digging through my closet, I find the box. Covered in stickers, it's filled with pictures, ticket stubs, cards (mostly from Elle and Amber), and a few strands of Mardi Gras beads. On the very bottom—my breath snags when I see it—I find the White Stripes jewel case, the CD inside snapped cleanly in half, blood still clotting its ragged edges. I haven't really looked at it and never used it to cut again. Not on purpose. It didn't seem right somehow.

I take out one half, old blood clotting its jagged edges. My desk lamp reflects a prism of colors off its underside, but instead of throwing a rosy warmth like the triangle, the colors feel cold. I drag one edge softly down my left arm, across my stomach, down my right. I leave no marks except soft lines that instantly disappear. I run the edge over my fingers one by one. Deadly, but only if I press down. I don't. Then I flip the jewel case and see his name still scribbled on its back.

Mom's knock startles me. "Kat, there's stuff for sandwiches if you're hungry."

"That's ok, I'm..." I start to say as I remember the afternoon. Last May, right before exams. He brought the CD in from his car. *It's cool because they're brother and sister. You should totally borrow it. Check out this one song...* Joey cared then, like we actually had something. So sweet, he wanted me to like his music. And I did. But even more, I liked him. Then, anyway. I close my eyes for a long second before I tuck the bloody broken half back into the jewel case, snap it shut, and drop the whole thing in the trash on my way to the kitchen. It takes my breath away a little, but screw it, I leave it there. "I'll be right there. A sandwich is fine." *Everyone knows they're not really brother and sister, you idiot.*

TWENTY-FIVE

I take three steps into chemistry and stop. Joey glares at me from a lab table at the front of the room, looking sullen next to Rodney Chu, Alberta Phun's girlfriend. Or boyfriend. I'm not sure what Rodney's going for today since he's sporting both a bow tie and fake eyelashes, but Joey looks supremely pissed.

Alberta sits in the back at my table and raises an eyebrow as I slide onto the stool.

"Soooo, looks like you blew crew season for Joey," she laughs, raising her hand for a fist bump. A few stools over Taylor gives me the finger.

I shrug and look down. I have nothing against Alberta, but I'm not in the mood. I actually think it's pretty cool that she does her own thing at Marshall, but I don't feel like dealing with anybody today. "It's ok," she whispers when Clarick starts taking roll. "I wouldn't want to talk about it either. Just so you know, not everybody is upset he's been benched. And that InstaChat...nasty damn flyer." I look at Alberta.

"He's benched? Like, for the *season*?" This is what I get for telling Elle and Amber I don't want to hear Joey gossip. I miss everything, even the important stuff.

"Yeah," Alberta says, "and supposedly a recruiter from some California college was scouting him."

"Miss Phun, can I help you with something?" Clarick's voice screeches from the front of the room. Alberta looks down and mumbles, "That's *Mr.* Phun to you."

"Excuse me? Did you say something?" Clarick glares from the whiteboard.

"No, Miss Clarick," Alberta says, sighing through the rest of roll call.

"Let's get our salt measured so we can test those ionic bonds," Clarick says from the front of the room with a grimace that might be a smile. I turn to Alberta.

"So, are you stuck back here for the rest of the semester? Is Rodney mad?"

"Nah, Rod's cool. I'm not sure what's going on but as soon as I walked in, Clarick was like, 'Ms. Phun, you'll be Kat Morgan's science partner for the remainder of the semester,' and then dragged Joey up there."

"Why?"

Alberta shrugs. "Who knows. I heard some freshman got caught with weed he bought off Joey, but it's probably because they don't want you two together. I guess Clarick wants him up front so she can watch him or something." Alberta tilts her head and gives me a look. "Would you still want to deal with him in class? After the InstaChat crap?"

I see Joey at the front of the room bent over his experiment next to Rodney, talking quietly. I *am* relieved I don't have to be his lab partner anymore, and Dad was going to make Clarick switch us around anyway. But seeing him makes me sad. When I see him like this, not trying to impress Taylor and just being himself—the guy who complimented my mom's lemonade, who shook hands with my dad—I remember why he's Pete's friend, why I liked him, why we once clicked. My heart twists at the thought.

Until I see him grab his notebook and start to take notes.

I'm startled to see him writing, probably because I've

never seen it before. He always claimed his handwriting was too bad to read and his typing was too slow so I should take care of the lab notes, all the crap you say to a sucker when you don't want to do the work.

After class, Clarick calls me up and confirms everything Alberta already told me: Alberta will be my partner until holiday break, Joey will be up front with Rodney, and that she expects my lab reports to come in cleaner and less wrinkled from now on.

She pauses by the door. "You know, Kat, sometimes people who seem special turn out to be…well, they turn out to be a lot of polish. A base metal all shined up. And shine eventually wears away." Without waiting for a reply, Clarick turns and squishes off to the faculty parking lot in her gummy shoes.

Not bothering to knock, I push through the outer door and into the studio, kicking leaves as I go. I can usually hear Tia's music from the driveway, sometimes even from my bedroom window. The sudden silence crawls on my nerves.

"T?" I look around. The furnaces are on but silent, turned way low. "Tia?"

"Hey, Kat! In the kitchen." I look through the half-door that leads into the kitchen and stop short. A guy sits at the breakfast bar, holding a mug. Scraggly blond hair curls around his collar and he's wearing a guy's version of Tia's uniform—dusted-up jeans, a t-shirt, and work boots. He's holding a mug and when he lifts it to drink I see a small, sexy scar near his chin that dimples. Damn, he's hot. As soon as I step into the kitchen Chloe zooms in and plants her huge paws on my chest, tackling me with a slobbery kiss.

"Hiya, Chloe! Um, hi." I wave at the guy and feel his bright eyes on the top of my head as I bend over to give Chloe belly rubs.

"Hey," he says, taking another sip. His voice is deep and dusky. "How's it going?"

"Good."

"Hey, Kat." Tia pops out from behind the refrigerator door holding a can of whipped cream.

The guy on the stool turns to me. "So *you're* Kat, the amazing apprentice. Tia talks about you all the time. Cool to meet you. Maybe later you can show me what you're working on." For a second I think he's messing with me. *Apprentice?* I'm about to point out that I don't know crap about glassblowing, that all I do when I'm not crying is make ugly ashtrays, but the look on Tia's face shuts me up.

"Kat's been an amazing help to Chloe and me these last few months. And she's a fast study." She smiles and passes me a fresh mug of cocoa, steamy with lots of whip. "So, Kat, this is Teddy. A friend of mine." I watch Teddy's eyes slide across the counter and land on Tia in a way that makes my stomach flutter. Teddy? Why do I know that name?

"Oh, hey, I didn't mean to bust in on you guys..." I start to back away into the studio when Tia gives me a look.

"Please. Get in here. Come look at this." Tia points at a laptop on the counter and I'm mesmerized by colors swimming all over the page. Ruby reds, golden yellows, velvety greens, and ocean blues all jam into one another in the most amazing pattern etched across a canvas that stretches across an entire warehouse wall.

"That's gorgeous. Is this at some museum?" I ask.

"It's mine," Teddy looks at me with his clear blue eyes, "in my studio in New York. Well, not exactly *in*. More like on the wall. I wasn't going for big but it did its own thing and, you know..." Teddy shrugs, "this happened. Kind of like how Tia's glass talks to her."

I stare at the gorgeous swirls of color.

"So you like?" The look on Teddy's face reminds me of a kid bringing home macaroni art for the first time.

"Totally. Amazing."

"Told you!" Tia says, poking Teddy in the ribs.

"Ok, ladies, I know Tia's got some Swedish overlay to work on," Teddy says, grabbing Chloe's leash, "so Chloe and I are going to head out. Hey, Chloe, want a walk?" Overjoyed at the magic word, Chloe runs at Teddy full force and wiggles.

Walking by, Teddy leans down and brushes his lips across the back of Tia's neck, making her shiver. Then he snaps Chloe's leash onto her collar, opens the door, and disappears while tucking an empty poop bag into his pocket.

"Oh my god!" Tia says, slapping the counter, "How was the dance? Tell me! Was it completely awesome? Did you guys have a blast?" I try to smile, but Tia's expression tells me I'm failing epically. I feel my face start to crumple so I stick my nose into my mug to soak up yummy cocoa smell.

"Ok, what happened. Something with the girls?"

"No." My voice breaks but I manage not to cry. "This guy I kind of dated last summer was wasted, doing drugs with this girl. Then they drove off."

Tia looks thoughtful. "Is this girl a friend?"

"God, no. I just freaked out because I didn't want him driving. The last time he did that really bad things happened. So I called Dr. Caleno and now they're in a pile of trouble and the crew team hates me."

"You still did the right thing."

"I guess. Um, so what's with the hot guy? Teddy?"

Tia walks past me into the studio without saying anything, going straight to the warmer to pull out a little log of bright red glass, which she starts to roll.

"Uh, Tia?" I'm still standing on the kitchen side of the studio.

"Yeah?" She starts rolling the liquid color on the metal table with her usual intensity.

"I'm just wondering what you're doing. With the red?" Tia stops and looks down at the gooey glass cylinder.

"The red? I have no clue," she says, bursting into laughter. "I've totally lost it." Tia sighs, deep and heavy. This sigh sounds different. Not the Chloe-needs-a-bathroom-break-and-my-hands-are-full-of-hot-glass sigh. Or even the Kat-made-another-hideous-ashtray sigh. No, this sound I definitely haven't heard before.

"Teddy. He's, um, staying here for a little while," she says before turning her own stunning shade of red.

"Yeah?" I raise my eyebrows.

"An old friend." Tia nods, turning even redder.

"That's right! You mentioned him before. He used to help you blow glass. I didn't know he was a painter." I put down my cocoa and snap on my goggles. At the oven I use the metal rod like Tia has taught me, taking my soft glass to the table and alternating between rolling and blowing, slowly and carefully.

"He just did gaffing to help me in the studio because my pieces were so heavy. And then after the accident...well, we just fell apart as a couple. He tried to be supportive, but sometimes you just have to figure things out on your own. But you already know that."

I stop rolling. "You guys were a couple?"

"Yeah."

"Obviously he still likes you. And he's so, you know, *hot*," I laugh.

"Before a few days ago I hadn't seen him in almost two years, since the day he walked in on me..."

"Walked in on you...like, with another guy?"

Tia looks at me like I've grown a second head. "God, no! He walked in while I was breaking my vases that night."

"Oh..."

"He didn't say much, but he did try to stop me." I try to imagine what it feels like to love someone so much I'd step between them and flying glass. "That's how he got that dimple-scar on his face. It was a crazy night. We never said it out loud, but we broke up right after that. We both knew."

Suddenly, Tia gasps. I stop blowing into the rod and look around, wondering what I've done. "What!? What's wrong?"

"Oh my god, look at what you did!" she says, pointing. I look down at yet another misshapen ashtray that I'll re-melt. *Except it's not*. On the end of my rod is a beautifully shaped sphere. A little wobbly, but actually pretty awesome. "Congratulations."

I look at my glass ball, and smile. "Yay, I finally made

a shape!"

Tia shakes her head. "No, sweetie," she says gently, "you finally let go." And when she folds herself around me with her bad-ass scar resting on my cheek, it feels scratchy and weird, but mostly it feels safe.

TWENTY-SIX

The leaden sky looks darker than even just an hour ago. Flurries fall silently and melt as soon as they hit the ground. Everything feels dark, grey, and hesitant. Seems kind of perfect. My eyeliner looks like crap from crying, but I can't do much about it now.

The hotel foyer shines like a penny, all white marble and blinding chrome. An easel by the elevators announces the 7th Annual NECOM gathering in the Godiva Wing. My stomach feels full of shards and I have a dull ache behind my right eye but I plaster on a smile and go in.

I scan the tables along the front of the room and finally spot Elle, looking deliriously happy, next to Amber who's talking to a tall serious-looking guy in a suit. Mr. Rockstad, ever the teacher, chats up some guys from St. Gabrielle's Prep who look itchy and uncomfortable in their suits. Cardinal Rule #4: geeks hate dress clothes.

Elle spots me first, excuses herself, and comes running up. "Kat! Ohmygodohmygodohmygod! Mr. Morito, the head of Sandblast, is *here*! He talked to me," she scream-whispers in my ear, pinwheeling her hands, "and wanted to know what place I felt hacking had in game design! Can you *believe* that? Then Amber and I had a really awesome conversation with these agents from Homeland Security's Computer Emergency Response Team. The one woman said she did her graduate work in defensible systems..."

I take Elle's hands gently between mine and look her in the face. "This all sounds incredible but you need to breathe before you hyperventilate."

"Hyperventilate? I won't hyperventilate!" Elle giggles like a third-grader and grabs me around the waist.

"How many lattes have you had today?"

Elle waves her hands. "I don't know. A few?" We lurch up to the table just as Amber

finishes shaking hands with Tall Guy. When she turns, she looks like she's just seen a unicorn. That talks.

"Federal Law Enforcement, Special Computer Division." She whispers in god-like awe. "He said our program has the potential to change the way hacking looks to network administrators." Elle squeaks in a pitch I've only heard once before during a concert.

"He. Said. *That?*" Amber nods and they grab hands.

"Wow, guys, that's really...sexy?" I half-laugh, feeling good for my friends. They've worked hard for this.

"You have no idea!" Elle squeaks. I look around at all the tables with their trifold poster boards and blinking, pinging laptops. Mr. Rockstad has moved on to the buffet table where two parents pepper him with questions.

"So, what happens now?"

Amber shakes off her dreamy look. "Well, the judges already got copies of all the programs a few days ago and they'll announce winners on the blog on Monday. The exhibit really just lets everyone meet and see what the competition is working on. Elle and I made our rounds about an hour ago."

"Well, ladies, how are we feeling?" Mr. Rockstad asks walking up, holding a handful of pretzels. Amber and Elle both nod with bright smiles. "You both did a great job today networking. Amber, I saw you and Agent Fournier speaking..."

I wave and sneak away to the buffet to grab a bottle

of water. Standing by a tabletop display of a giant spider made entirely of old hard drives, I sip my water and face the inevitable. Pete's going to flip out. Like Incredible-Hulk-flip-out. I wonder if Tia would let me sleep in the studio or one of her bedrooms for a few days. At some point, I need to tell Amber and Elle. I don't want to ruin their day, but the last time I saved bad news, things sort of blew up.

I walk around the room looking at students' posters and browsing vendor booths. As I snag some freebies—a Sandblast sticker and a SafeData! Frisbee for Chloe—I begin to wonder about some of the more obvious problems.

Are we going to be one of those two-holiday houses now? Or do we have to pick which parent we want to spend our holiday with? What if Pete and I disagree? Or, worse, what if the other parent has to spend the holidays alone?

As I come full circle back to Amber and Elle's exhibit table, I realize I haven't asked myself the biggest question of all: what if, when Dad moves out at the end of the week, *he's happier away from us?*

Mr. Rockstad and some other advisors speak to the judges, two older men in bow ties and a woman in a crisp suit, while Amber and Elle and the rest of the room begin to pack up their equipment.

"So, this is it? You just pack up now? I feel like I missed most of it, you guys. Sorry I was kind of late."

Amber turns with a tired smile. "I'm glad you came. It wouldn't have been the same if you didn't. Now hold this bag." She begins filling a tote with three-ring binders and handouts. "Oh, hey, what are you doing tonight?

We're going to get pizza and hang at my place."

"You guys, um..."

Elle nods as she slips her laptop into a case. "Yeah, you should totally come."

"Well, I *would* but..."

"Wait." Amber's crinkle comes popping out on her forehead. "What's wrong?"

"Um..."

"*Kat*, what's wrong?" Amber stops what she's doing as Elle looks up.

"My dad. He, uh..."

"He what?" Amber asks.

"Um...my dad's moving out. My parents are separating. He told me today while Mom was at the bakery." I look away, willing myself not to cry. Not here.

"*What?*" Amber's eyes pop wide.

"Are you ok?" Elle folds me into a hug. "What did Pete say?"

I roll my eyes. "He doesn't know yet."

Elle holds me at arm's length. "They haven't told him?"

"Nope. That's going to happen tonight. And I'm really not looking forward to it."

Amber flips her mane of hair down and comes back up with a thick ponytail. "Your parents need to deal with Pete on their own, which is why you're coming over."

"I don't know."

"Just call them from my house. You need to be out of there tonight. Ask Dr. Caleno. I bet she'd agree." I wipe my eyes and force a small smile.

"Ok."

I call right after the pizza comes but before we start the movie.

"Hello?" She sounds stuffy, like she's been crying.

"Mom? I'm at Amber's and, um, I'm going to sleep over." Silence. "Mom? Is that ok?"

"Dad said he told you today."

"Yeah. He did."

"Are you ok? Do you need to come home? Maybe you should come home." I hear her voice break.

"I'm fine, Mom. I'll be home tomorrow."

"I'm sorry, Kat, this isn't what Dad and I wanted. But sometimes things happen..."

"I know." More silence.

"And, honey, please don't...*you know.*"

"What?"

"Don't do anything."

"We're just eating pizza, Mom."

"I know, but just promise me you'll avoid sharp things. Don't fall into an unsuccessful

coping pattern." Holy crap, she is not serious.

"Mom," I take a deep breath, "I'm going to go now."

I hear her blow her nose. "The blog says that girls often turn their stress inward and..."

"Mom?"

"Yes, Kat?"

"I love you. Goodnight."

TWENTY-SEVEN

"Hey."

I freeze and say nothing, letting my bag slide from my shoulder to the floor as kids rush by trying to beat the last bell before homeroom. Ignoring him, I step up to my locker, spin my combination, and grab what I need. Joey's hand curls around mine as I reach for my physics textbook.

"Look at me, Kat." His hand shakes. He smells like coffee. I look up, briefly, into blue eyes I already know and look away.

"Don't."

"Kat. *Please.* Just look at me." I pull away and finish shoving books into my bag. I reach around, feeling blindly for my locker door to close it. I don't want to look at him. His hand curls under my chin, rubbing a soft spot right above my necklace before lifting my face to meet his. I turn away. And then I don't.

"Homeroom bell is going to ring." I look straight at him and can't decide what I see. Shame? Hope?

"I know. I don't care. I need to talk to you," he says, suddenly moving closer so there's no space between us anymore, no space to breathe. He hasn't been this close to me all year.

My heart catches as his fingers brush my neck, moving slowly towards my face. His touch still feels magnetic and soft and I forget, for just a second, the rough way he shoved me out of his car at my house that night, the slick blood and guts that painted the headlights, the rotten death and guilt that shove into my dreams every night.

I shudder. This, whatever this is, shouldn't be happening.

"Stop..."

Joey looks surprised. "But I have to talk to you."

"Not interested."

"I need to find out what's going on." I say nothing, only shoulder my messenger and move to get past him. "Look, people are pissed because you went to Hunter, but that's not my fault. I don't even know how this all started. All I know for sure is that my crew season is completely screwed." He spills it out in a rush, as if the words won't come fast enough.

"No kidding people are talking about me. I'm sure it has nothing to do with the InstaChat post!"

"Yeah, I saw it."

My mouth falls open. "Really, Joey? You saw the post *that you uploaded?* Real shocker."

"What? No, I didn't." I just look at him. "Seriously, Kat, I didn't do it!"

"Then who did?"

"I don't know."

I try again to walk away but this time he grabs me and pulls me in. Too close. "I swear to you, I didn't make it."

"It was your picture..." I start to say, but then realize with a sinking feeling how stupid I'm being. He took the picture, but that means nothing. Anyone could have made it and uploaded it. I even said that to Principal Hunter. "Forget it. It doesn't matter..."

"Listen to me. I didn't make the flyer and I didn't," he stops to look around as he lowers his voice, "force anything on Paula at the dance. Why would you tell

Hunter that?"

I look into a face so open and clueless, I almost wonder what I've done.

"Kat, you don't get it, he *called my parents*. He said he had to, that it was a legal obligation. Then my parents had to get a lawyer and talk to Paula and her parents. Now I'm not allowed to see Paula, Coach thinks I lost a recruitment spot, my mom won't look at me..."

"I'm sorry your crew season is ruined and everything's screwed up. I really am. But this isn't *my* fault." His eyes start to water, like he's about to cry, but then his face flashes anger as he runs his hands through his hair, making the short blond bits stand on end.

"Paula wanted to party. I didn't *force* her to do anything. Why did you tell Hunter that?"

I bite back a scream. "That is not what this is about *and you know it*." Joey winces at my hiss. People rushing to homeroom slow down to watch. A few point and click with their phones, evaporating any chance of keeping this private. An obnoxious Spirit Slut texts furiously. My words hang in the air between us.

"Damn," he says quietly, shaking his head, "you're still pissed about *that*? I can't believe you ruined my crew career over some old dude who probably got up and walked away." The soft words hit me so hard I feel punched in the face.

I grab the front of my locker for support, but there's nothing there to hold me. I slide to the floor.

Joey crouches down. "Do you need the nurse or something?"

I look at him and take in his blue-eyed gaze. The pain and guilt of all these months washes over me: the way my stomach twists thinking about the car's graceful slide right before the crunch of bone; shoving away my best friends; working over my body into something hideous I couldn't recognize so I wouldn't have to look at myself.

Somewhere in the back of my brain, it registers that the hallway has gotten quiet. Too quiet. Homeroom bell has rung. Amber will wonder where I am. On cue, my phone vibrates.

I struggle to stand. I have to go to the front desk for a slip, but what will I say? *Well, Mrs. Caine, I hooked up with the guy I crushed on last summer but then we ran over an old guy, who I thought we killed but weren't sure about since we didn't stop to check so...can I please have a late pass for homeroom?* Joey looks at me expectantly.

"We missed the bell," I say lamely, leaning against the cool metal of the locker.

"Yeah, I know." Joey slides down next to me. We can't get caught like this. Aside from already being in trouble with the front office, the gossip alone would kill me. "I just don't get it," he says quietly, unbelievably believing I have screwed him over. He still hasn't heard me. Not last summer, not now.

Maybe it's time.

"We were wasted and you ran over that man. Then we drove away." I take a shaky breath, "His blood was smeared all over the car when I got out. I found out he's ok, but it was wrong. *Really* wrong. Nobody walked away except us." My eyes never leave his face. I watch the words sink in, spin around, and cloud his eyes with doubt. His gaze flitters—to the ceiling, to the floor, along the hallway—until it lands back on me.

He shakes his head. "Shit. You really don't remember,

do you?"

"Of course I do," I sniffle. "I said we should call 911 and you wouldn't."

"Kat...you said your dad would kill you, and you thought we'd get expelled or worse."

"Whatever. We should have called 911." For the millionth time, I struggle to remember. That thing about the expulsion, yeah, maybe I did say that, but still. Something eats at me, something I am forgetting...

"You were afraid it would ruin your chance with NECOM and you'd never be allowed to go to Quantico if they found out. So we switched seats and I drove you home. *I drove you home* because you couldn't stop shaking, you were too fucked up. You made me swear I'd never tell."

What he's saying can't be right. *It can't.*

I remember music spilling from the stadium into the backseat where I was floating, flying. Leaving the show and sliding smooth and slick through the night, headed to the secluded spot near the jogging path where everyone goes to screw around. And I remember the thud, the blood...and, oh my god, the pavement under my bare feet as Joey yanked me from the driver's seat and dragged me to the passenger's side, shoving me inside, slamming the door. Jamming down on the gas. Peeling away.

I remember.

I reach out to touch Joey's shoulder and he jumps as if I'm electric. Maybe I am. Maybe I'm a thousand watts of pure pain, ready to infect anyone I touch with horror and grief.

"I have to go," he says, hunched under a weight that is now mine.

TWENTY-EIGHT

I glide across the room, somehow skirting the mounds of books, clothes, and CDs scattered on the floor. The air smells funny, like something sweet and burnt, and I wonder if Mom is testing a new recipe downstairs instead of at the bakery.

My chest of drawers yawns open, and fear pulses through me. Has Mom found the triangle and taken it? How could she know? I plunge my hands into the drawer and root around, dripping a rainbow of panties and bras onto the floor that add to the messy mix of clothes already blanketing my carpet.

My fingers catch and close over it. I pull it out into the light, expecting the usual orange and red of a juicy grapefruit or blistering sun, but when I hold it up to the window I see that the light has drained from the day. A fat moon slices through my curtains instead. When I look at the art glass backed by the milky light, the colors don't shine but instead look murky and brown around the edges, like dried blood. I'm surprised to see the same rusty brown color streaking my legs. Have I have gotten my period?

Dark liquid runs down my arms and stomach too. I lift my hand and feel wetness along my jawline, on my cheeks, in my hair. Rivulets of brown blood snake down my body.

Joey stands by the door, looking at me, crying, shaking his head. I grab my phone and try to dial for help, to call Amber, to text Elle, but I can't. I forget my friends' numbers. I remember my dad's friend from Piccollo's. *Margie*, Dr, Caleno said. I look in my phone for

Margie, scrolling through contacts until I realize I don't know her. Dad never introduced us.

What time is it? I'm going to be late for homeroom. I need a note. How will I get a note? *Joey*, I turn to the door, *we're going to need late passes* but Joey is gone. In his place lies a picture strip from the photo booth. I look but see no pictures, only shadows and smudges.

I open my mouth to call for anyone—Elle, Amber, Mom, Dad, Tia—but nothing comes out. *Maybe I'm dead.*

"No, Kat," Dr. Caleno says, a shimmery form in the doorway, blood red wings hanging quiet by her sides. She steps into my room, carrying with her a radiant blue light that softens the sharp edges of my room and lights the dark corners. "You've never been more alive."

My stomach drops before I'm completely awake. The sheet snarls around my arms and my pillow feels wet from sweat. Today will definitely suck.

I stand outside the Webers' and let the cold sweep away the last remnants of my dream. Through my breath I see the white picket fence that defines our yard from the alley. Ahead of me the Weber's garage, a tribute to beige vinyl siding, sits at a slight angle to their driveway. A sad line of wilted blue irises, long ago dead from the cold, lean against the fence. Bright leaves float through the alley on a cold wind, creating a sharp blanket of color against the tired brown dirt.

Just a few more steps. I have to do this. My stomach flips in protest. I reach the studio, give a little knock, and push open the door. The room feels unusually cold.

"Tia?" No answer, but this could mean anything. She might be wearing headphones, be upstairs or in the kitchen, a million different things. The worst feeling, I realize, is not feeling strange entering somewhere for the first time, but feeling like a stranger in a place that has become like a home.

This unnerves me, and breaks my heart.

I step back. I'll come back tomorrow. Or later. Or...never.

"Kat?" Tia swings the top half of the kitchen's Dutch door open. "What are you doing?" I don't answer her, just stand in the open garage door, letting leaves wrap around my feet before they scuttle into the studio and across the floor. "You ok?" Tia comes to stand in front of me. "Honey, what's up?"

Before I lose my nerve or puke, I reach into my jacket and pull out the orange triangle. I walk across to the steel table where we roll glass and put it down. I won't be rolling anything in here anymore. No hideous ashtrays, no beautiful spheres, nothing.

The triangle's colors seem dull against the metal of the table, not something worth stealing. I reach out a shaking hand to push it further onto the table and stroke it, just once. My breath catches and I turn to face my friend.

Tia comes and looks at it curiously. "Hey, you found one of those colored shapes I made way back. Remember that? It was one of your first times in here, I think. You leaned on the rolling cart and trashed the whole pile!" She giggles. "So where'd you find this?" She picks up the triangle and looks at me. She's going to be *so mad.*

I force myself to look into her green eyes. "I took it. That day I broke the stuff. I'm so sorry. I...needed it." I watch Tia's face go from confused to something I can't read at all.

"Needed it for what?" She looks the same way she did the day I met her, holding herself tall, tattoos peeking through her t-shirt, scar standing out like a warrior's mark.

"It's beautiful."

"Yeah, it's a nice orange," she says drily, "so what did you need it for?" Her eyes drill into me.

"I wanted to use it for cutting," I whisper, curling my arms around myself as I stare at the floor. When I finally look up, I find Tia slumped in her chair at the patio table, head in hands.

"T?" She rocks her head back and forth in her arms, saying nothing. "Tia? Please. You're freaking me out."

She lifts her head slowly, eyes clouded. "I'm freaking *you* out? So sorry. Forgive me." The sarcasm hurts, but it's not like I haven't earned it.

"Well, thanks for," I spin my hands around, "all of this. It's been great and I'm just, I don't know...sorry." I head for the door.

"Are you kidding me?" If Tia looked mad before, now she's furious. "You come into my studio—my home—steal from me, hurt yourself *with my art*, share confidences with me for weeks, and now you're going to just say 'I'm sorry' and *leave*?" Her scar, an angry red against her paleness, only adds to the crazed effect as her firecracker red hair spills every which way from its ponytail.

She stomps over, work boots swirling up puffs of batch dust, smearing her tears. "Didn't you learn *anything* from Elle and Amber about friendship?"

I stand silently. I don't know what to say. I never do. Tia grabs my jacket and tugs me back towards the table.

"Show me," she says stonily.

"What?"

"Show me. I want to see *exactly* what you did to yourself with my glass." I could refuse. I could get up, leave, and not come back to this garage ever again. She won't be here forever, just until the spring when the Webers return. I consider this. Then I stick out my hand.

"I'm serious, Kat. I need to know. I have to see." Her voice breaks. I put my thumb in her face.

"I popped my thumb." I see her wince. "I did this *by myself*. You are not responsible. *I am*. I'm so sorry. I'm sorry I took it and I'm sorry this hurt you." Because, I finally see, my actions damaged a whole lot more than just my thumb.

"Your arms?" she asks tentatively.

"No. Just my thumb. The glass was too beautiful. I looked at it a lot though."

"So why give it back now?"

"I don't want it anymore," I say, but we both know that's a lie. "Actually, it's more that I don't think I should have it since it's not mine."

Tia nods. "Ok." She pauses. "Look, I know things have been tough for you, between your parents' problems, that guy, the InstaChat bullshit, all of it. And I appreciate that you gave this back. I do. But not because I care about a piece of glass, because I care about *you*. Knowing you took this to hurt yourself...knowing that breaks me in half, Kat."

"I know." I move towards her but she turns away.

"This is really and truly messed up," she says, shaking her head. Suddenly, the garage door bangs open and we're both tackled by Chloe with ice-cold, extra-slobbery kisses.

"Hey, ladies," Teddy says as he unzips his coat and shakes flurries out of his hair. He stops, noticing our faces. "What's going on?"

"Teddy, could you maybe..." Tia says, gesturing towards the door. He looks confused.

"Could I what?" he asks, standing there awkwardly, coat hanging from one arm.

"I need you to go, uh, to the store. For hot chocolate."

"Hot chocolate..."

"*Please*," Tia says, losing patience. Teddy nods, and starts climbing back into his jacket.

"Got it. Hot chocolate, because *that* makes sense," he says as he heads back out the door.

"You need to go too," she says turning to me.

"I'm sorry. I really am, I promise..."

"I know, Kat. I know you're sorry. I just...I need to think about this. Ok? Don't freak out, but I need some time. Please."

Standing in the cold, flurries sticking to my tears, I watch Tia bend down and give Chloe a kiss on the head before she looks up, shakes her head, and nudges the door closed with her boot.

TWENTY-NINE

"Grab your shit and let's go." Pete snatches his car keys off the kitchen counter and heads for the back door.

"What?" I put down my toast and look up.

"I said, let's go." I open my mouth but shut it when I take in his rough stubble and tired eyes. I don't even remember the last time I've seen him at home. Was it Sunday when I got home from Amber's, or maybe Monday? Come to think of it, since I started hanging out at Amber's after school again to do homework, I haven't seen anyone in my family much.

"Go where? Dad's coming over this morning." It sounds lame, even to me, but I don't care. I want to see him. He moved the last of his boxes during the week and promised to stop by around lunchtime today. We all know Mom's Sunday schedule at the bakery, so it's no accident he's coming over while she's out. Besides, I have a physics chapter to plow through.

Pete looks grim. "No, he's not. Something about his transmission, so we're going to his place. I don't care if you come or not but I'm leaving in five, so don't bitch if you miss the ride."

I brush my teeth, throw my physics books into my messenger, and shrug on a Marshall High sweatshirt over the long-sleeved tee I've just slept in and jeans I swiped off the floor. Hopefully I won't see anybody I know.

I haven't ridden with Pete in practically a year but the Cherokee looks about the same. Sports drink bottles litter the floor, along with gum wrappers and diet soda cans, probably Meghan's. Her smell, cigarette smoke overlaid by something sickly-sweet, sticks to the seat. If I had bothered to worry if Pete would still give me a hard time about Joey, I shouldn't have since it obviously won't be a problem. Whipping out of our neighborhood, Pete cranks the radio so loud it rattles the ancient Jeep's dashboard. I want to ask him how he knows where to go, if he's already been to Dad's new place, but after looking at his tired, angry face I skip it.

The ancient wipers smear grimy snow across the windshield as we take Lancaster Avenue through downtown Wayne and head towards Paoli. Dad's apartment complex, a set of large brown buildings tucked back in the trees, sits in the middle of a sub-division. My stomach sinks when we turn in at the battered Oaktree Acres sign. The weathered wood makes it seem like an old-age home.

Suddenly this all seems too real. I push away Dr. Caleno's voice telling me to remember what to do with automatic thoughts, how they lead to feelings that make me want to cut. Yeah, whatever. Instead my fingers itch as I do a mental inventory of my messenger. I've got books, a few pens, gum, my phone, lip gloss, keys, maybe a pencil. I don't know for sure what might be on the bottom, but I can hope for a paperclip.

We park and I follow Pete down a slushy sidewalk lined with trees, turning onto one of the footbridges that cut deep hallways between the brown-shingled buildings. Pete steps up and knocks on door #42 while I walk to the back stairwell.

The view grabs my breath. Although impossible to see from the street, the development sits nestled into the side of a steep slope. While the front-facing apartments get stuck looking at the parking lot, those in back overlook a shallow valley bursting with trees loaded down with a dusting of snow and fiery leaves that haven't fallen yet. A hawk screams and swoops into a dark stream.

"Hey, Pete, you made it! Where's..." I turn towards Dad's voice. He peeks around the doorway, deep wrinkles grooving his tired eyes. "There she is. You like the view, Kitkat?" He comes outside to stand next to me, rubbing his arms against the cold.

"This is amazing, Dad. Really nice. Really...peaceful." My voice breaks on the last word.

"Come here, honey. It's ok." He rubs my back while I sniff and snot into the cold. "It's going to be ok." I figure it's easier to nod than ask what that means. "Let's go inside."

I cringe as soon as we walk in the door. Pete already lies splayed across a squashy sectional couch I don't recognize, playing something gross and bloody on a new PlayStation 4 at a volume that makes my ears bleed.

"Hey, champ, we're going to turn this down for a minute," Dad shouts, leaning over and grabbing the remote. Pete shrugs and keeps playing while I look around. "Make yourself at home, Kat." I notice how anxious Dad looks and I know he's trying, that this is just as weird for him. "How about some coffee?"

I nod and wander around the room, eventually peeking into a tiny closet, a bathroom, a large bedroom tucked down the hallway, and a medium-sized room with a desk and some other office furniture I haven't seen before.

"It looks like you raided Ikea, Dad," I say walking

back into the kitchen as he pours my favorite brand of whole coffee beans into the grinder.

"Yeah, you might say that. I didn't want to disrupt the house so I figured I'd just buy a few simple things and make the place comfortable."

"Sure, especially since it's only temporary." I know I shouldn't push, especially since he's only been living here, like, five minutes, but I can't help it. He says nothing as he grinds the beans, measures out filtered water, and gets the coffee brewing. Then he pulls half a dozen flaky croissants from a grease-stained sack and puts them on a plate.

This stabs at me as I remember the early days of Mom's bakery, back when she'd taste-test cookies and pastries on us. Croissants were always Dad's favorite, a special thing she'd bring home long after we ok'd the recipe...until, one day, she didn't anymore.

Dad settles down on one end of the couch while I sit on the floor against an ottoman, my rabid need for a paperclip pushed back behind other, more nagging thoughts. I watch Pete play his gory game, ignoring us, and wonder what he's thinking. I'm not even sure what we're doing here. How truly weird to visit someone who used to live with you, who told you to clean up and be home by midnight, just last week...

I grab a croissant, take a sip of coffee, and dump my physics book and notebook onto the floor, where my lab note printouts fall from between the pages.

We determined the behavioral properties of magnetic fields using iron filings and a magnet. Our hypothesis asserts that magnetic forces, as applied to poles and fields, can be demonstrated by showing how like poles repel and opposite poles attract...

Too bad Mrs. Victoria from English lit isn't here to point out the irony. I shred my cuticles as I think about how pissed I've been, how I spent the summer and fall avoiding Dad and hating him for hurting Mom and being so crappy to me the night of the concert.

Now I want him back. Something clicked the day he saw the flyer. I could see that all he wanted to do was save me—from Joey, who he believed wanted to hurt me, and from myself, which he could never do, no matter how much he tried. I wonder if he even knows this.

What happens when our magnetic poles get broken? When random crap makes us repel the people we should be holding on to?

"What's her name?" I blurt. I breathe slowly and try to steady the mug in my shaking hands as a few drops of coffee hit my notebook. Dad looks up from the Sunday paper, startled.

"What's that?" I can see a string of red blossoming under his collar, slowly moving up his face. He knows exactly what's happening even if I barely do.

"Your girlth...girlfriend. The one in Amsterdam. What's her name, Dad?" My heart beats like a hammer pounding a broken nail—unsure, unsteady, and way too loud.

Dad looks at me straight on, unblinking. "Her name was...is Iris." The air sucks from the room as I see the irises leaning against our fence, planted by Mom in a warmer season, now drooped and fading in the face of winter. "And we're not seeing each other anymore."

I stare at Dad, willing him to break open and tell me he's lying, that he loves her and is leaving for Europe. But he doesn't do those things. Instead he puts aside his paper and coffee, moving to stand in front of the windows that overlook the valley.

"The separation is about taking time and space to figure things out with your mother." Dad turns. "I know that sounds ridiculous, but it's true. Your mom and I are starting counseling next week.

"Mom has her own things to say to you, so I won't speak for her except we think it may be good to have you both come to a few sessions. I know you have your own counseling, Kat, but we're hoping you and Pete will think about it." Dad squeezes his mug so hard his knuckles turn white. "I won't promise what I can't guarantee, except that it's over with Iris. That's done."

Dad runs his hand through his hair and looks over at Pete. "What do you think?"

Our experiment with magnetized iron filings further proved that, in the vicinity of a magnetic field, a moving charge will experience a force.

My brother, the cockiest jerk I know, sits quietly, game controller limp in his lap.

"Ok," he whispers.

"Ok," I say.

"Ok then," Dad says, nodding, wiping his eyes. "Ok."

THIRTY

So...weird. Instead of the squishy green velvet couch, in front of Dr. Caleno's desk sits a straight-backed chair. Something out of a throne room or medieval dungeon, its metal back and arms make me shiver. As I sit, a sad heaviness wells up inside me, like I'm weighted down inside a wet coat I'll never be able to take off.

"What's with the electric chair?" I joke, trying to shake off the sorrow suffocating me.

Dr. Caleno looks up from her papers.

"How are you today?" she asks, ignoring my question, all business. "Have you thought any more about sharing the accident with your parents?"

"But you said I could decide when to tell them," I say, panicked. I am so not there yet.

"You can..."

"I'm not sure there's enough counseling in the world to make me ready for that."

Dr. Caleno looks at me. "I think you're a lot stronger than you think." *Strong?* I cry at nothing, get stressed at everything, lie to my best friends, have a brother who hates me, and a dad who supposedly just broke things off with his slutty girlthing.

"I don't feel strong."

"No?"

"No way. Most days...I don't mean to whine, but most days I feel like crap," I say, sliding down into the depths of the chair.

"Have you driven again since the concert?"

"What?" I half-laugh and hold my breath. What the hell?

"Have you?"

Dr. Caleno's eyes flare as she leans forward on her desk. I feel my breath swept away.

She knows.

My voice clicks in my throat as she comes around her desk, walking slowly.

"Own it," she says, her voice flat and cold. "Now." She rises in front of me, too tall, furious, majestic, terrifying. I squeeze my eyes closed and fight for air as her breath boils over my skin. "Taketh that which is yours, Katherine."

My chair tips back and I windmill my arms forward, catching nothing but air.

I see the moon, a dirty half-slice in the sky. A small dog strains on his leash. He dashes into the park as blacktop, rough and wet, cuts my palms. I'm on my knees, trying to stand when headlights speed forward, coming towards me. I have to get up, move, do something but the car lights fly at me, too fast, dizzying. I am going to die.

When the car bumper connects with my head, I fly backwards, hands dragging and bloodied on the road, legs twisted under me, back snapping, eyes rolling. I see nothing but a screaming red, followed by searing pain.

Raised voices break into my pain, an argument gets heated, then quiets.

"The kids at this school...they're mean." I recognize Dr. Caleno's voice, but it sounds thicker, deeper.

"Kids have always been mean. Now they just have really good tech." The accent sounds cool and soft like a summer afternoon. A guy.

"I know. And good technology makes it all easier,

especially the indifference. This is the high price of free will."

"Would you want a world without free will?"

Silence.

"Trust me, you'd hate it. Now stop this."

I see volcano blasts and hot rock, sun beating down on a scorched, brittle land dead of anything except a breeze that flutters dozens of black wings.

Then, light.

I open my eyes and smell blood. Dr. Caleno's calico, the same one that's always eyeballing me from her window seat or, I now realize, following me around town, sits a few inches away, washing her paws, watching me as I lift my face from the carpet. Dr. Caleno holds out her hand. I wave it away. Stagger to my feet. Pull the monstrous chair upright and slump into it.

"I was driving that night," I say quietly, blood from my nose dripping onto my hands. "But you already know that."

Dr. Caleno nods, handing me a tissue. I wipe my face, trying not to smear blood everywhere.

"Am I crazy?" I ask. "Is this all real?" The calico, bath finished, jumps into my lap and starts to purr.

"I can't tell you what's real or not," she says.

"I saw things..."

She nods again.

"I swear I wasn't lying to you. I only remembered the other day, with Joey, when he told me. Then it came back. *I* drove that night from the concert. It was *me*." I choke on the last word.

"So what now?" I sniffle. "Am I going to jail?" The panic I've managed to keep snuffed finally—blessedly—

rises up.

"We'll need to talk to the police. And your parents, of course."

I nod. "That'll give my dad something to talk about. He told me he's going to start counseling with Mom..."

"How did that conversation go?"

"Does it matter?"

"Sure it does. How did talking to your dad make you feel?"

"Don't you already know, with your superpowers or whatever?"

"Not superpowers, Kat. This is just me. Here to help."

I feel queasy. "Is my life always going to be like some failed chem lab experiment?" I blow my bangs off my sticky forehead.

"What do you mean?"

"Just that nothing is simple." Truth is, I feel better. But so what? Things are still a mess. A huge one actually.

"How do you feel when you cut?" She asks it so quietly, I hear the calico's tiny, whistling snore from my lap where she's fallen asleep.

"I don't know." We both know that's not totally true. "I feel in charge. I feel full."

"Full?"

"Yeah, like I can do anything. I feel good. At least right then. Not so much later."

"Right. If it didn't feel good in some way, you wouldn't do it."

"I guess."

"So you can either use replacement activities, like we've talked about, or you can not need to replace it anymore, so it goes away."

"I seriously screwed up."

"Yes, you did. But there's tomorrow."

Her words fade into the dusk spreading through the room. We sit in shadow, silent, the setting sun throwing everything into relief against the walls while smoky blue light pours in from the skylight.

THIRTY-ONE

Slamming the Jeep door, I see Amber and Elle climbing out of Betsy right next to me.

Elle looks over and raises her eyebrows. "No way!"

I juggle my bag, trying not to spill my mocha latte. "Pete has a stomach bug or something. So when he begged off I told Mom that since he was sick, he wouldn't need the car. She couldn't really argue with that. Plus..."

"You didn't tell them yet," Amber says. I nod.

"Not yet. Maybe tonight. I don't even know how to start." We wind our way through throngs of cars towards Marshall's front doors when we see Principal Hunter standing by the entrance.

"What's with Hunter?" Elle asks, shifting a laptop bag I haven't seen before higher on her shoulder.

"Hey, is that new?" I lean in for a closer look. "Nice."

"Yeah, it's from..." she hesitates oddly, "my dad. To celebrate NECOM."

"What's wrong?" Something about the way she's looking at me makes me cringe.

"I'm so sorry, Kat. About your dad. And now the whole concert thing." Elle looks as if she's about to cry.

"Elle, I don't expect you to stop saying the word 'dad' just because mine moved out. And I'll deal with the accident. Not much choice there."

Amber sighs. "Enough with the sad. Come." She points to benches at the side of the building, tucked just out of sight where the Stoners sometimes hang out before last bell. Today it's deserted, probably because it feels like ten below.

"We'll be late—" I start but she cuts me off.

"We won't. We have at least ten minutes before homeroom and these are going to get gross sitting in my locker all day," she says, shaking a donut bag, "so let's have breakfast."

We crunch through brown weeds, brittle and frozen from frost, to the bright blue benches where we watch our breath make swirls in the morning air. I feel, not for the first time, that it all used to be a lot simpler.

Elle slips her mittened hand into mine. "Has your mom talked about your dad at all?"

"No. After Pete and I went to see him last weekend, she wouldn't say anything. And now Pete's acting weird." I watch a fat robin land a few feet away and start pecking the brown grass.

"Weird how?" Amber pops a donut hole while clapping away the powdered sugar.

"I don't know. Just acting bizarre, like he won't say anything."

"And that's bad?" Neither Elle nor Amber have ever liked the way Pete talks to me.

"Not bad *necessarily*," I say, "I just feel better when he's being a jerk because then I know the deal."

"Supposedly he and Meghan had a fight in the caf yesterday," Amber says. I hadn't heard about the fight but it made sense.

"He let her calls go to voicemail while we were at Dad's. I thought it was because he was busy playing his bloody zombie game, but maybe they're breaking up."

"Or maybe this thing with your dad is kicking his ass," Elle says, surprising all of us. The idea of *anything* knocking Pete out of his stupid jock attitude seems unlikely but, then again, I couldn't have predicted much from the last six months.

"I don't suppose you guys have figured out Thanksgiving yet?" Amber asks, mouth full. Before I can answer Hunter appears around the building, obviously looking for somebody.

"Kat Morgan," he says, from the edge of the walkway, "I need you in my office." I grab my bag and stand, suddenly tired, as I watch the robin make one, final stab at the ground and take off, a juicy worm hanging from its beak, completely helpless.

Bonsky worries a thread in her cardigan until it starts to loosen the button. I want to tell her to cut it out, that she's on my nerves, but that won't go over well. Today Hunter looks extra-dapper-dork in a lavender shirt with matching purple tie covered in little red lobsters. Perhaps Mrs. Principal Hunter dressed him. He pushes around papers, sighs, and delivers the big news while he rubs his face. Bonsky makes little noises while shaking her head and *tsk tsking* around her mint.

"Ok, Mr. Hunter. Thank you for letting me know." I stand to go, trying to digest it all.

"And, Kat, if your parents want to discuss this further, please have them set up an appointment with me through Mrs. Caine."

"Sure thing." I walk out the front office and bump into Madame Jolais.

"Bonjour, Kat. Comment va-tu?"

I hold out my hand and make a so-so gesture. "Comme-si, comme-sa," I say.

Madame raises her eyebrows and smirks. "That good, huh?"

I lay my hall pass and late excuse on Ms. Wu's desk and slide into an unfamiliar seat towards the back. Busy with a commentary on magnetic forces, she nods and continues her lecture, gesturing so that her arms flash shadows across the projection. I'm doing much better in class, but today even Ms. Wu's enthusiasm leaves me flat as I hear Hunter's words: "...*in light of events, Mr. Lawlor has made alternate accommodations for the remainder of his junior year.*"

I didn't bother asking if he'd be back next year. He won't. Joey's gone, transferred out of Marshall High. And it's my fault. I wonder if Pete knows. Does the rest of the team? Principal Hunter wouldn't say where he's going, just that it would take effect immediately. Joey didn't want to wait for spring semester because he felt that would "exacerbate the issues."

My bag starts buzzing and I rush to turn off my phone. The only teacher more excited than Mr. McCallister by Marshall High's zero tolerance policy on phones is Ms. Wu. Pretending to dig around in my messenger, I check my phone and choke when I see a text from Shelley, two rows up and three over in our usual seats towards the front. I'm stunned, but not just because she's in Ms. Wu's direct line of vision.

did u hear? Js gone!

Question answered. The crew team knows. Shelley looks back at me. How am I supposed to answer? I turn off my phone and suffer through physics until I can beg off a nurse's pass for my morning classes. I brace myself for chemistry that afternoon, but Joey is conspicuously absent from Rodney's lab table up front.

"Hey, how's it going?" Alberta asks, making a last-minute change in smudgy pencil to our lab report. Clarick won't like that but I don't say anything.

"Um, ok?" After Clarick takes roll and we set up for our next experiment, I finally ask. "Have you heard about Joey?" I force myself to stop fiddling with my pen after I flip it across the aisle, right into Adam-the-AV's head. I need to calm down. No one has said anything to me. Then again, I spent the morning hiding in the nurse's office.

"I heard he was transferring because he thinks his recruitment chances are messed up. He'll probably go to St. Paul's since they have a Division One varsity crew."

My eyes widen. "How do you know that?"

Alberta shrugs. "Which part?"

"All of it."

"I know St. Paul's has a D1 rowing crew because I used to date someone on the women's team and I know about Joey leaving because, *hello*, it's all over school."

"I know he's transferring but...why?"

"*Why?* You're seriously asking that? You did dime on the guy."

"I didn't mean for any of this to happen. No wonder everyone hates me."

"First of all, that's not true. And secondly, you can't worry about what the garbage people say. Take it from someone who knows." I consider that for a second.

"People are going to say I ruined crew season, that his leaving is my fault. And it's basically true."

"Maybe," Alberta says, distilling a dark liquid into a beaker. She puts down the glassware and leans in. "You may not realize it, but you gave him a big fat present.

Transferring will save his recruitment chances. And maybe next time, he won't be so quick to get wasted and blow off a dance where he's being worshipped when *some people* who don't look like perfect little boys and girls aren't even allowed to attend." She smiles at my shocked face. "Just sayin'."

THIRTY-TWO

I grab the last bin and lug it inside, being very careful not to tip it. Mom has already begun displaying her cupcakes on their special corner table surrounded by sprays of exotic flowers and towering pillars of petit fours. I know we have to work fast to avoid the wedding planner who wants us gone before the rehearsal dinner guests arrive.

The candy maker, creator of all the beautiful red, gold, and orange petit fours, and obviously pissed, shouts something in German to her assistant. Then she stomps over to eyeball Mom's salted caramel cupcakes covered in fondant sculpted into little tuxedos, and grunts. When she walks away I catch Mom's eye and we burst out laughing.

"What was that about?" I laugh as I finish unpacking the rest of the cupcakes. Mom giggles.

"Who knows. Maybe she forgot her huge wooden spoon." I'm surprised. Mom usually stiffens up during event prep, saying things like, "We have to make a complete impression, and not just with the baked goods, blah blah..." I understand that but it's a lot more fun helping her when she's calm and not flipping out. I figured she'd be a mess when her assistant, Patty, called out sick but she seems fine, almost in a good mood.

Helping also gives me a legit excuse to miss GamerCon. I made such a mess of that whole deal by piling lies, letting Amber and Elle go without me feels more honest.

"Kat, be careful! You almost knocked the whole thing over!" I've accidentally bumped a few of the petit fours onto the table from one of their stands.

"No big, Mom. They're fine."

"Do you want to tell *her* that?" Mom whispers, tilting her head towards the door where the candy maker blasts her assistant with a string of loud German that sounds a lot like cursing.

"Ok, got it." I scoop up the tiny pastries and quickly arrange them back on their fancy piles.

"Where's the voile?" Mom starts rooting around the bags and bins at her feet.

"Right here." I hand over a large bag stuffed with fabric that Mom winds in and out of the cupcake stands. Sheer lengths of frothy orange, red, and brown billow around fifteen dozen cupcakes—some wearing little tuxedos, others in orange cream covered by white fondant wedding dresses—and hundreds of the chocolate maker's delicate petit fours. When we stand back, the table looks amazing. Mom takes a deep breath.

"Excellent," she says. "Do me a favor and take a picture? Then let's get these bins back in the van. We can..." but her voice is drowned out by the wedding planner, a tall, thin man in a light blue suit who holds his head and whines.

"But, Louisa, I *told* you the bride and groom do not want dark chocolate in the fountain. And certainly not 70% cacao! They want milk. *Milk*!" The chocolate maker stands like a massive tank, arms crossed over her huge chest, brushing off her apron and pretending not to hear.

Mom and I pack faster, piling our empty bins and bags onto a rolling cart. I try not to laugh while Mom gestures to keep packing. We head out a service entrance just as Louisa starts cursing again in German. When I look back she's swinging a large chocolate spatula at the planner who looks slightly terrified.

We stuff all the empty bins back into the van and blast the heater.

"We've got until 10:00 when we'll come back and break down," Mom says. I nod. I've helped before and I know the routine. She sits behind the wheel for a second.

"You want to get something to eat?" Mom pushes her hands into her gloves and looks hopeful. I don't have the heart to tell her I'm not really hungry, that I scarfed half a package of Pete's Oreos before we left. Usually his hoard, the cookies have been sitting in the cupboard for over a week, untouched. For some reason, he doesn't seem to want them anymore.

"Yeah, sure."

"What are you in the mood for?"

"I don't know. Do you want to," I can't believe it even as I say it, "see if Pete wants to come?" I have zero interest in dinner with Pete but he's been so weird lately I'm surprised Mom feels ok ditching him. Unbelievably, I almost feel sorry for him.

"Oh, Pete has dinner plans...with your father." Mom looks away and busies herself with the rearview mirror as she pulls into traffic.

"Um, ok."

"I hope that's alright?" Mom says this in a way that sounds like she's about to cry.

"It's cool, Mom. I'm fine with it. Why wouldn't I be?" I stare at my mittens. Something definitely feels weird.

"I don't know. Ok, so where should we eat?" she says too brightly, deflecting the question, pretending we haven't just been talking about something important. I hate it when she does this. "I hope the Daleys enjoy the orange cream. I used more of a sweet orange essence this time because when they came to the tasting they both said they wanted to shift the flavor profile slightly. Patty called them 'hipster foodies' and I didn't even know what that meant so I said—"

"Mom, what's going on?" She stops her chatter mid-sentence. We've only been driving a minute but she makes a sudden turn into Midtown Cross Shopping Center, pulls up by Lucky Larry's Diner, and cuts the motor.

"Let's just have some dinner..." She fumbles with the keys to avoid looking at me. I shake my head.

"Mom, we are seriously not eating at Larry's. What's wrong?"

She hangs her head. "I'm so very sorry for all of this." She blinks fast to keep the tears back, but a few drip down the front of her ski jacket anyway. "Pete is very unhappy about the separation. He's...he's not handling it well." No kidding. I could have told her that. Normal Pete does not blow off Meghan, stay home sick, hand over the Jeep without a fight or an insult, and quit partying, all in one week. "We're concerned, so your father is talking to him tonight about...possibly having him move into the apartment."

"*Pete's moving in with Dad?*" I wouldn't have guessed that one.

"I don't know. Maybe. But just temporarily. Only for a little while." Mom sounds panicked. She sniffles and wipes her eyes. "We knew he would take the separation hard." Everybody at school knows something's up with Pete, but I don't say this to Mom. "And then Dad and I were worried you might start hurting yourself even worse when you found out, but we had to tell you. Your father couldn't just move out and not tell you."

She pulls off her gloves and clutches the steering wheel like she's holding a life preserver. "This is all such a mess. I don't know how to make this right, and I don't know what to do to help you."

"There's nothing *to* do, Mom. Just leave it alone. You and Dad obviously have your own stuff to figure out."

"How can I leave things alone when you hurt yourself? *When you cut yourself open when you get upset?* You don't understand, you're not a mother!" she sobs. I'm trying to remember the stuff I just went over with Dr. Caleno so I can say something shrink-like, but all I hear is the sound of my head hitting the blacktop while being dragged and...god...

"I know you say you're figuring it out, but Dad and I, we've been scared to say anything and we want to help. We don't know how this all even started..."

Even though we can see our breath in the van, the air crystalizing around us, I suddenly feel hot and feverish, my skin burning itself inside out. Dr. Caleno's words slice into me again, demanding I take what's mine. Mom and I have never talked about the concert.

"Mom..." my voice shakes, "you know the night of the concert?" The Oreos churn in my stomach as I think again about the locker conversation, Joey walking away.

"Yes." Mom looks startled. "What about it?"

I take a second and steady myself. "I was driving."

"You were driving where?"

"Home. I was driving home and..."

Mom shakes her head. "I still can't believe you were

drinking with that boy after everything we've said about…"

"Mom, stop." I hold up my hand. "After the show. I was driving. I had an accident. Then Joey switched places and drove me home."

Mom's eyes, red-rimmed and puffy, look huge in the dark. "You had an *accident*? What accident?"

"Mom, *I hit somebody*." My voice breaks. "A man. He's ok but…I did it. I hit him."

"I don't…" Mom shakes her head, leans over, and holds me. "My god," she whispers, smoothing my back. "My god."

THIRTY-THREE

"I can't believe he's actually *going!*" Elle lets the curtain slide back over the window and drops to the floor next to her iced tea. She shakes her head, reaching for more chips.

"And your mom's not totally losing it. Well, more than usual anyway," Amber adds, as she balances her history book on one knee.

"I know, right? Like everything else isn't bad enough." We all get quiet at that. My stomach flops at the memory of my mom, dad, Dr. Caleno, and me sitting at the police station, filing a report. I hear the front door open and close for the hundredth time, and a soft tread on the stairs. Pete's almost done moving his stuff into Dad's car when we hear the ear-splitting screech of feedback.

"Someone might want to tell him he should unplug from the amp before he starts moving his guitar." Amber rolls her eyes.

"You know where his room is. Help yourself," I say. Amber puts aside her book, gives her salty hands a quick swipe on her jeans, and disappears out of my bedroom.

I look at Elle. "I was kidding!"

Elle dumps her books and gets up. "I have to see this." I shake my head as I get up and follow her into the hall. We tiptoe down to Pete's room, which has fallen quiet. I peek around the door and see Amber propped on Pete's bed, chatting while she noodles on his unplugged guitar. Pete drops beaten up sci-fi novels into a storage bin.

"...and so when it was too complex to make all of the

components in the second program run, we stuck with the first and they liked it," Amber says.

I haven't been in Pete's room in years. The last time may have been in 8th grade when he sent me to get his phone off his dresser. It hasn't changed much. Posters dot the walls and some dirty clothes sit in piles on the floor. A crew magazine splays out on his desk over a math book.

"Good luck. That'll be cool if you win."

Pete looks up when Elle clears her throat in the doorway. "Hey, Elle. Come in if you want." Elle sits next to Amber on Pete's bed.

"Are you taking all that with you? Are you sure Dad has room?" I point at the container.

"No, it's for Goodwill or whoever. Just cleaning out..." We watch Pete flip through old books and drop them, one by one, into the bin.

"So, are you excited to be moving?" Amber asks carefully. I'm not sure anyone has asked Pete this. He shrugs.

"I guess." He drops in a few more books and then looks up. "Actually, not really. Just a place to crash until I can figure out what to do."

"But you're finishing out the semester and then coming back to Marshall in the spring?" she asks. I look at Amber. It hadn't even occurred to me Pete might transfer schools. Not in his senior year with one semester left. Who does that unless you absolutely have to? *Like Joey.*

"Yeah, I'm coming back. I'm not changing addresses or anything."

Elle climbs from Pete's bed. "Well good luck with the

move and everything. See you around the cafeteria."

Amber takes the hint and follows. "Yeah, see you, Pete," she says, moving into the hallway. We head back to my room and as soon as I close the door I hear my name.

"Be right back, you guys," I say and dash back down the hall. Pete sits on his bed with his hands in his lap.

"What's up?" I ask, poking my head in.

"I wanted to tell you...you fucked up when you went to Principal Hunter about Joey."

I hold up my hand. "Totally not having this conversation."

"Just let me finish," he says impatiently.

"Then finish. I have to study." Pete looks at me with dark eyes. "You have three seconds and I'm gone. I'm serious."

"Ok, just chill for a minute." He picks up his guitar, puts it back down, paces to his closet, and turns to me. "Joey didn't make the InstaChat upload."

"Does it really matter anymore?" I stuff my hands into my armpits so he can't see them shaking.

"Yeah, it matters. Going to Hunter really screwed Joey. He and Paula had been serious and that whole thing with the recruiter, that ended right there. Man, it's *hard* to score a crew recruiter when you're only a junior."

"Thanks for the lecture," I say as I turn away.

"I did it," he says. "I made it."

I say nothing, just stand in the doorway as Pete picks at a flake of tape on the wall that used to hold a Flyers poster. Or maybe it was Metallica. I can't remember. I can't really breathe. I hold myself so still I swear I can see my heart beating through my hoodie.

"Hey, Champ, the car's packed," Dad yells from

downstairs. "Mom says we'll be eating in about fifteen. Kat, you can see if the girls would like to stay…"

Pete and I say nothing. He turns to look at me, and I know I should leave now. Just go to my room and call it good. But I can't. I uncross my arms, push my bangs out of my eyes, and step into his room.

"Why'd you do it?" I ask, shaking.

"You wrecked varsity. Totally screwed us up. The dude used to *like* you, Kat, and you basically ruined his life." I feel a sharp tear in my heart knowing he could be right. But as much as I want to crucify myself, to find one more excuse to carve the hate out of my body, Joey and Paula shouldn't have been driving. As bad as I feel for getting them in trouble, no way should either of them have been near a car.

I swear under my breath. "I can't believe you would do that to me."

Pete sits at the foot of his bed and pushes around the book bin with his foot. "You broke up the team."

"Fuck the team!" Maybe Pete taking a break from living here, from being around, isn't such a bad idea. "And fuck you!"

I realize, too late, that I'm yelling. Mom and Dad stand behind Elle and Amber in the hallway. Everyone looks shocked and silent, unsure what to do.

I push past everyone and head down the hall.

"Kat," Amber whispers, following me, "we're going, ok? Call me later." They give me quick hugs and slip into my room to gather their books and leave.

Dad goes into Pete's room. I can't hear what he's saying but I know that tone, the same he used on me the night of the concert, a combination of controlled fury and hurt. Mom stands in the hallway, eyes too bright, looking at me.

"Kat..." she comes down the hall, pulling me to her as Dad hefts a bulging bag full of Pete's workout equipment into the hall and down the steps. Pete squeezes past me with his guitar. He won't meet my eyes.

"We'll be discussing this, Peter," Mom says, quivering, furious.

"Yeah," he says to the floor. He stops at the top of the steps and looks at me. "Later, Kat."

THIRTY-FOUR

I step into the studio and stop when I hit a wall of music so loud it makes my ears bleed. Tia and Teddy lean over the workbench, turning the most enormous vase I've ever seen.

Teddy catches my eye and nods from his spot where he steadies the huge potholders made of newspaper as Tia rolls the body of the vase back and forth. I know that even with much smaller pieces Teddy's job is hard, hot work. He nods to Tia and she stops, resting for a moment before Teddy directs a stream of water at the connection point where the vase and rod meet.

With a sharp twist and snap of the huge vice pliers, the vase drops gracefully into Teddy's outstretched hands. I see his legs bend under the incredible weight. He places it upright on the metal table where it towers over their heads. I roll the receiver dial down to a reasonable volume as I walk by, making Tia snort.

"That's...wow," I say as I gawk at the new vase. The piece stands almost a full five feet above us on the table, putting me in complete awe. The colors create the illusion of staring into a living volcano making it impossible for my eyes to know where to rest. Swirls and patterns run and chase each other with such a fierce intensity, they snag my breath.

I grab Tia's hand and squeeze it. "It's amazing. I don't even know what to say."

Under a layer of silt and ash, a sheen of sweat, and wild, loose curls, Tia looks at me. "How are you feeling?" she asks. I try not to look so shocked, knowing how supremely pissed she's been at me.

"I'm ok. Good. Pete moved out."

"I saw," she says, nodding her head. "That must have been weird, huh?"

I screw up my courage. Again. "Tia, I'm sorry for..." but she cuts me off.

"You upset me, Kat, I won't lie. But here we are. And," she says, turning to the huge vase, "you are here for the inception, the moment this new piece becomes part of the collection. Welcome to Outliers, Redux."

I'm startled out of my awe by a wet nose sliding across my arm, trying to burrow into the brown bag I'm holding.

"Did you bring doggie treats for everyone, Kat?" Teddy asks.

"Ha, Chloe wishes. This is coffee, Tia, from my mom. She said you'd like this hazelnut." My mom may have sent the coffee, but right this second it feels more like a peace offering.

"I swear, if you go home riotously sick, I will not be held responsible," Tia says. I just smile through my chips and nod.

"What are you talking about? This spread is fit for a king!" Teddy booms, shoving the rest of a frozen burrito in his mouth. The assortment does look a little odd: burritos, peanut butter, protein bars, pineapple cubes, potato chips, leftover takeout Chinese noodles, and hazelnut coffee. "Actually, you know what I could really go for?" Teddy's eyes light up.

Tia looks skeptical. "I can't even fathom. Scrapple?"

"You'd let me bring meat in the house?!"

"Not even close. Forget I even joked about it." Tia

wrinkles her nose.

"I really want...Oreos!"

I make a choking sound. "Gah! Absolutely not. No Oreos. I've already eaten, like, an entire bag since Pete swore them off."

"You think your mom might..."

"Teddy, my god, we're *not* asking Margaret for Oreos! Eat another burrito. Or a string cheese." Tia shoves food across the table at him. She sips her coffee and looks thoughtful. "Speaking of Oreos, how's Pete doing at your dad's?"

"He seems ok. I guess he's getting used to being there." I fiddle with the bag of chips, trying not to think too hard about my family's messes.

"Your mom was so upset by the whole thing but she did a good job being supportive of Pete's decision. That must have been hard."

"He basically freaked out when Mom and Dad told him about the separation. It's not like I was happy about it, but I kept it pulled together. Mostly anyway."

"Yeah, you did, but you have Dr. Caleno. From what you said, Pete felt like this extra-special guy. Imagine having that belief about yourself, and then being unable to deal with news your little sister handles just fine. He felt horrible *and* embarrassed."

"Why are you sticking up for him?" I cross my arms.

"I'm just trying to help you understand why the guy is falling apart and so pissed at himself about it."

The idea that Pete feels embarrassment, maybe for the first time in his charmed life, hadn't occurred to me. Obviously, if he hadn't been such a tool to begin with, he wouldn't have been so shocked to feel crappy like the rest of us.

Tia puts down her mug, and drills her green eyes into me. "So how goes it with you?"

"What do you mean?" I know, of course, exactly what she means.

She rolls her eyes, but only a little. "With the counseling, Kat. With Dr. Caleno. Business as usual?" In Tia speak, 'business as usual' means I am going to my sessions, completing my journaling, and doing my best to swap other hobbies instead of slicing myself up.

I smear peanut butter on crackers one by one, and stuff them into my mouth. I know I should tell Tia about the accident, the police report I finally filed, the whole disgusting mess, but Dr. Caleno said I should follow my gut on when. The words feel stuck in my throat, so I go with easy instead. "Business as usual. Dr. Caleno wants me to garden."

"Garden?" Teddy takes his nose out of his second burrito. "You want help? My granddad always gardened. I am *the* soil master." Both Tia and I stare.

"Soil master?" I ask. "Do I even want to know?"

"You *absolutely* want to know. Hold on," Teddy says as he pushes back from the island and disappears upstairs.

Tia looks amused. "I have no idea what that's about."

"He can help me if he wants but if he's only staying a few months, he won't be around to plant stuff in the spring." I get up to refill my coffee and grab Tia's mug as I go. When I look back, she still hasn't spoken.

"Tia?" I stop when I see the tears sliding down her face. She swipes at them with an ashy hand, leaving batch tracks across her pale skin. I sit down and push her mug towards her. "Are you ok? Are you guys...breaking up?"

To my complete wonder, she busts out in a laugh.

"No, we're not breaking up. Total opposite. Teddy is staying, as in, moving his studio down here to Pennsylvania. And I'm terrified. We tried this before and..."

"So you might be getting *married*?!"

Tia looks like she might vomit. "What? No. I did not say that..."

"Well, he's moving in and it's the opposite of breaking up!"

"Who's getting married?" Teddy asks, standing at the bottom of the steps, half-eaten burrito in one hand, seed catalogs in the other. Tia holds her head.

"Stop, stop, stop. No one is getting married!" she yells at the ceiling as I start laughing so hard I choke.

"Now, honey, I'm sure *someone* out there is getting married. And why are you crying? Oh, you gave it to her!" Teddy turns to me. "Do you like it?" Turning a funny color, Tia jumps up, grabs Chloe's leash, and walks Teddy to the door. "I did not *give it to her*. Now go. Go."

"Uh, I need a dog," he says, mumbling through the last of his burrito.

"*Chloe! Walk!*" Tia screams so loudly I almost drop my coffee. Chloe, confused but happy, comes bounding down the steps and into Teddy's arms. With Chloe and Teddy bundled and out the door into what looks like the first snow of the season, Tia sits. Instead of taking up her mug, she takes my hands.

"Kat, remember when I introduced you to Teddy and I said you helped Chloe and me so much when we moved here?"

"Sure, it was really sweet of you to say that. I thought I was in the way actually..."

"You weren't in the way. You've never been in the way. We love that you're a part of our lives. And I meant what I said. You did help Chloe and me. The way you were so open about everything," Tia takes a deep breath, "...especially my scar. It didn't scare you."

I roll my eyes. "Of course it didn't. I have a couple of my own, you know."

Tia nods. "I know. And that's why I have something for you."

I clap my hands like I'm five years old. "The sphere! You put a loop on it!"

Tia gives me a look. "You said you wanted to learn how to do that yourself."

"Oh, I do, I just...I love presents!" We both laugh as she pushes a box across the table at me. Small and wrapped in tissue with a red bow, it could be anything except my glass sphere.

I pick at the ribbon gently and peel away the tissue until I'm holding a little gold box. I lift the lid, gasp, and close it again.

"This can't be right," I whisper.

Tia nods. "It's right, Kat. Nothing has ever been more right." I reach inside the box and lift out my treasure, sides buffed to a soft frost, top swinging from a black waxed cord pulled through a tiny drilled hole.

My orange triangle.

My ruby red sunset.

My reminder.

I cup my orange sunset in my hand carefully,

differently than the way I've held it so many times before. The glass, soft and smooth, slides gently against my palm. No edges to cut or slice. As Tia puts the cord over my head, her scar gently brushes my cheek. I barely understand what this all means, but I'm trying.

"Um, Tia, I have something I want to tell you. About me...about what happened this summer..." I say quietly.

THIRTY-FIVE

Dr. Caleno's muted conversation stops midsentence when I enter her office. Her phone sits across the room, untouched on one of the plant stands, and she's alone.

"Talking to the cats?" I joke, even though I don't see them, not even the calico. I'm only a little surprised. I've finally figured out that things aren't always super-normal in here.

She watches me flop onto the green velvet couch—it's back in its spot, replacing the hideous throne thing—and slide down into it.

"So who were you talking to?" I ask, just to see what she'll say.

"My boss," she says between sips from her coffee mug.

"Oh. I didn't think you had one. You have your own business and everything."

"We all answer to someone, Kat, even if we think we don't."

"I guess." I fidget, thinking about my dad. And the weird afternoon ahead of me.

"You look serious," she says.

"My parents are freaking out. They don't know what to do about everything. Pete finally moved out and obviously now they're upset about...you know," I say, spinning my hands around, not wanting to say it.

"The accident?"

"Yeah." I nod.

"What's happening with Pete?"

"He did it." Dr. Caleno raises her eyes at my words. I suspect she already knows what's coming, but I say it anyway. "He made the InstaChat upload."

She says nothing at first, just taps her pen on her temple, looking thoughtful and shrinky. Then she surprises me by turning away to look out the window behind her desk, the big round one that makes the field behind her house look like it sits in a picture frame.

"He told you this?" As if she didn't already know. She knows everything.

"Yeah, the other day. But he apologized and said he regrets it, that he'll never do anything like that again." That gets her attention. She spins around so fast papers fly off her desk.

"He did? He said *that*?" she asks, looking dazed.

"Yeah, right. Like he'd ever do that…so why didn't you just tell me?"

"Kat," she says leaning forward, eyes beginning to flash, "It was not my information to tell. If Pete told you he made it, then he decided it was time for you to know. I have nothing to do with it."

"I guess." I find that hard to buy. "Things really suck."

"I know you're nervous about your community service." Dr. Caleno comes around from her desk and sits next to me, letting the sofa envelope her too. "It'll be fine."

"I dunno." After watching my dad's face break the first time when Mom and I told him about the accident, and then watching it break again while Dr. Caleno helped me file the police report, I don't know how to feel. Judge Mega, the scary old guy who spoke to my parents, agreed with Dr. Caleno that I should do community service. This means I'll be scooping cat poop and walking dogs at the animal shelter for three afternoons a week until I'm 80 years old.

I hope the people there don't hate me. I don't know how much the judge told them...

"They won't hate you, Kat. Just do the work, help out, be yourself," she says, reading my thoughts in a way that still kind of creeps me out, even after the things I've seen.

"I have something to show you," I say.

She looks amused as I pull Tia's gift from my pocket, the orange triangle swinging on its black cord like a pendulum. "Wow," she says, admiring it, "those colors..." She holds it towards the window where the triangle grabs the light and reflects a chilly sun back onto her face.

"Have you ever heard of Custody of the Eyes, Kat?" I shake my head. "In old times it meant to keep your eyes down to see what was in front of your feet. Mostly so you didn't misstep or trip. Now it refers more to people who pay attention to things they need to see."

She folds the triangle into my palm and points at the window behind her desk. Unlike Tia's rough calluses, Dr. Caleno's fingers are soft and light like silk, but strong and steady too. "Use your custody of the eyes."

I walk behind the enormous wooden desk and lean against the window. Holding the pendant, I look outside through the small triangle of brilliant glass.

"What do you see?" she asks.

I see the field bathed in orange because I'm, duh, looking through orange glass. Nothing too shocking there, until...first there's Chloe and Tia, walking together, quietly. Then Pete lying on Dad's couch, staring into space, looking worried and a little sad. Elle and Amber, smiles shining, and Mom and Dad, sitting silent and close, but not touching.

Then...an old man holding his head, leg twisted under him at a funny angle. Pain and fury. Guilt and shame. Dying light and the coming night.

I turn to Dr. Caleno. "I see...everything."

"I thought you might," she says, smiling the way Tia does even when I make a mistake.

And I feel my heart crack open, maybe just a little.

EPILOGUE

"Your little bomb maker is here," says Dane, dropping the curtain.

"*Dane!*" Lily's eye get wide.

"Sorry," he laughs, holding up his hands, "Your next *patient* is here." Lily rearranges the folders on her desk and puts her phone on vibrate.

"Do you see the cats? I'm pretty sure he's allergic."

Dane snorts.

"Please, no commentary. The poor kid gets the sniffles every time he steps in here so if you see any of them..." Dane looks around and shoos Introit and Kyrie, the gorgeous but crabby calico and the tiny brown tabby with the soulful eyes, from behind a potted fern into the hallway and back towards the kitchen.

"All set. Hey, how'd things go with the cutter? Kathy?"

Lily takes a deep breath. "Kat. Well...there's a lot of smoldering pain there, and self-inquiry takes time. But she'll make it."

"Agreed. You know, she reminds me of Olivia." Dane catches himself when Lily stiffens. "Ooooh...I shouldn't have said that."

"No, it's fine. She reminds me of her too, for good or bad." Kat may still be a work in progress, but she won't go sideways like Olivia. No way. Although the whole Seattle mess pretty much insured that Lily would end up with high school kids again. No shocker there. Dane pulls Lily from her chair and wraps his arms around her the way only a best friend can.

"For good, Lil. Always," he reminds her.

"Thanks," she says, her quiet breath stirring only a handful of black feathers floating in the air as a tall, skinny boy with glasses steps timidly through the office door.

ACKNOWLEDGEMENTS

Writing is, by nature, a solitary activity. But don't be fooled. Those of us who write do it successfully only because an entire village props us in myriad, weird, gorgeous ways, big and small. My deepest thanks to my publisher, Nick Courtright, who gets it, my awesome editor, Alexis Kale, who makes me laugh between revisions, and all the fine folks of Atmosphere Press.

Some people support us without even recognizing how much their kindness means: Samantha Withers Lynch and Shannon Penston Kelly, thank you for listening, cheering me on, and being so kind. Stacy Saar, thank you for caring through the happy, the sad, and the gloriously difficult...

A huge thanks to Dax and the kittens; you are all my light, breath, sun, and moon. And finally, thank you, Momma. I'm sorry you're not here to see this because you've always been my biggest fan.

ABOUT ATMOSPHERE PRESS

Atmosphere Press is an independent, full-service publisher for excellent books in all genres and for all audiences. Learn more about what we do at atmospherepress.com.

We encourage you to check out some of Atmosphere's latest fiction releases, which are available at Amazon.com and via order from your local bookstore:

Katastrophe: The Dramatic Actions of Kat Morgan, a young adult novel by Sylvia M. DeSantis

On a Lark, a novel by Sandra Fox Murphy

Ivory Tower, a novel by Grant Matthew Jenkins

Tailgater, short stories by Graham Guest

Plastic Jesus and Other Stories, short stories by Judith Ets-Hokin

The Quintessents, a novel by Clem Fiorentino

The Devil's in the Details, short stories by VA Christie

Chimera in New Orleans, a novel by Lauren Savoie

The Neurosis of George Fairbanks, a novel by Jonathan Kumar

Blue Screen, a novel by Jim van de Erve

Come Kill Me!, short stories by Mackinley Greenlaw

The Unexpected Aneurysm of the Potato Blossom Queen, short stories by Garrett Socol

Gathered, a novel by Kurt Hansen

Unorthodoxy, a novel by Joshua A.H. Harris

The Clockwork Witch, a novel by McKenzie P. Odom

The Hole in the World, a novel by Brandann Hill-Mann

Frank, a novel by Gina DeNicola

ABOUT THE AUTHOR

SYLVIA M. DeSANTIS has been writing since she was a kid. Her books include *Watercharms: Ocean-Reiki Meditations* and *Academic Apartheid: Waging the Adjunct War* as well as essays, shorts, stories, poems, and articles for publications like Chicken  Soup for the Soul®, *Summer Shorts* (a middle school anthology), and *Youth Imagination Magazine.* She even wrote Goth fiction for a while...

Sylvia graduated from Villanova University with a B.A. in English and from Virginia Tech with an M.A. in English and a concentration in Women's Studies. She's currently busy combining two passions—education and alternative healing—into a suicide prevention campaign she is developing through her company, Compassion University. She also loves her cats. A lot. Visit her at sylviamdesantis.com.